the gossip file

ANNA STANISZEWSKI

sourcebooks
jabberwocky

Published by Sourcebooks Jabberwocky, an imprint of Sourcebooks, Inc.
P.O. Box 4410, Naperville, Illinois 60567-4410
(630) 961-3900
Fax: (630) 961-2168
www.jabberwockykids.com

Library of Congress Cataloging-in-Publication Data

Staniszewski, Anna.
  The Gossip File / Anna Staniszewski.
    pages cm
  Summary: Rachel Lee has looked forward to relaxing for two weeks at a Florida resort
with her father, but when his girlfriend asks her to help in a cafe, Rachel adopts a "cool"
new persona, Ava, to fit in with her older co-workers, until they ask her to help with
their Gossip File.
  [1. Gossip--Fiction. 2. Conduct of life--Fiction. 3. Popularity--Fiction. 4. Fathers and
daughters--Fiction. 5. Dating (Social customs)--Fiction. 6. Single-parent families--Fic-
tion. 7. Waiters and waitresses--Fiction.] I. Title.
  PZ7.S78685Gos 2015
  [Fic]--dc23

2014030985

Source of Production: Versa Press, East Peoria, Illinois, USA
Date of Production: November 2014
Run Number: 5002740

Printed and bound in the United States of America.
VP 10 9 8 7 6 5 4 3 2 1

Also by
Anna Staniszewski

The Dirt Diary

The Prank List

My Very UnFairy Tale Life

My Epic Fairy Tale Fail

My Sort of Fairy Tale Ending

For anyone who's ever wished to be someone else.

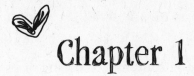

Chapter 1

"Rachel, how many rocks did you put in this suitcase?" Mom asks as she drags my luggage out of the back of her dented minivan. Evan, my too-cute-for-words boyfriend, rushes over to help ease the ancient bag to the curb in front of the airport terminal. The suitcase used to belong to Mom, back when she still traveled to places other than Connecticut to visit her sister.

"Here you go, Booger Crap," Evan says as he brings the bag over.

I'm so used to his goofy nickname for me that I don't even roll my eyes this time. Instead, I give him a shy smile and say, "Thanks."

When Evan grins back at me, his green eyes don't twinkle like they usually do. We're both pretending that me being away for two weeks won't be a big deal, but it stinks that I'm leaving when things are finally good between us.

Plus, I think he's been gearing up to kiss me all week. But I guess that will have to wait until I get back from visiting my dad in Florida. I seriously doubt my first kiss is going to happen at the airport in front of my mom.

Oh my goldfish. What if that's what Evan's planning? My mom will *never* let me live that down! My hands are shaking as I grab the suitcase and hurry through the parking garage.

I don't slow down until I get to the airline check-in counter. I've been trying not to freak out about the idea of traveling by myself, but seeing all those strangers with suitcases makes my nerves go into overdrive. With my luck, I'll accidentally wind up in Omaha instead of Orlando.

Mom must notice that my eyes are about to pop out of my head because she puts her hand on my shoulder and asks, "Are you sure about this?"

I push the ball of fear as far down into my stomach as I can. I've been dreaming of going to Disney World with my dad since I was six years old. I can't pass that up just because I'm scared of flying alone. "Yup. Chances are I *won't* die in a fiery plane crash, right?"

Mom shakes her head. "Is that supposed to be comforting? By the way, I checked the weather report in Florida this morning. It's going to be near a hundred degrees." She wipes her forehead as if the very thought is making her sweat.

"It was ninety here the other day," I point out. "Besides, I'm sure Dad has air-conditioning."

Okay, Florida in the summer might not be ideal, but with school starting in a few weeks, it'll be nice to finally get a vacation. I've spent all summer working for my mom's cleaning business, taking pastry classes, and organizing baking competitions (not to mention pulling pranks on people and making a general mess out of everything). It'll be a relief to hang out by the pool, relax, and spend some much-needed quality time with my dad.

Evan hangs back while my mom and I go check in at the airline counter. We stand in line for a few minutes until the ticket agent waves us forward without even looking up at us.

"What's your destination today?" he drones.

"Omaha," I blurt out, handing over the flight confirmation my mom gave me.

The man finally glances up at me. "What was that?"

"I mean Orlando," I say. "Orlando! Where SeaWorld is with all the whales!"

He raises an eyebrow and then looks at my mom. "And who's this?"

"I'm her mother," Mom jumps in. "I'll be escorting her to the gate, so I believe I'll need a pass to get through security."

The man takes her driver's license and studies it for a long time. Then he looks at Mom again, and I can tell they're coming, the words that always make my stomach clench into a ball.

"She doesn't look like you," he says.

"She's my daughter," Mom says, putting a protective arm around me. "But she looks like her father. He's Korean."

The man nods, but I can tell he's still not sure about us. Does he think my mom stole me or something? Or that because I don't have blond hair like she does, that means we're trying to sneak her into the airport?

Just when I think my stomach might clench itself into a black hole, the man sighs and grabs my suitcase. Then he hands me an enormous badge that I have to wear around my neck. It practically screams *UNACCOMPANIED MINOR FLYING ALONE*.

Finally, we get to the security checkpoint. That means it's time to say good-bye to Evan.

As I shuffle over to him, it hits me that I haven't thought through this dropping-off-at-the-airport plan. When Evan volunteered to come along, I was excited that he wanted to see me off like a real boyfriend would. I didn't consider the fact that he's going to have to ride all the way back to his house alone with my mom. What on earth will they talk about?

"So," he says. "I guess you have to go now, huh?"

I nod. "They're going to start boarding soon."

"Well." He looks down at his sneakers. "Text me when you land so I know you got there, okay?"

"I will."

When he glances up at me, I suck in a breath. He has a total "I'm going to kiss you" look on his face. This is really going to happen!

But wait. My mom is *right there*. Even though she's not looking in my direction—probably to give us some privacy— it still feels like her eyes are lasering into me.

Evan takes a step forward, and I start to panic. What do I do?

"If you need something to talk to my mom about on the way home," I find myself saying, "ask her about music from when she was a kid. She won't stop babbling for hours."

Evan's forehead crinkles. "Okay. Thanks for the tip."

Gah! Why does this have to be so awkward? Why can't I be brave like my best friend Marisol? She'd kiss the guy and be done with it, no matter who was watching.

"Anyway," he adds. "Have fun. I'll—I'll miss you."

My face goes hot. "I'll miss you too," I whisper.

And then I feel it. Evan's face inching toward mine. The scent of peppermint on his breath and the heat off his skin getting closer and closer. My mind goes blank for a second. I can't believe it. My first kiss is really going to happen… in front of my mom!

Just as Evan's lips are about to brush mine, I jerk my head sideways. All Evan's mouth finds is my ear.

Holy poached watermelon. Evan Riley tried to kiss me. And I turned away!

He coughs and steps back. "Um, so have fun," he says, his face flushing bright pink.

"I–I'm sorry. It's not…with my mom here…"

Why did my stupid head have to flinch? So what if Mom's right there? She's not even watching! This could have been the perfect moment, and I ruined it!

Maybe I can fix it. If I lean in and kiss him, then every-thing will be okay. *Do it*, I tell myself.

"Rachel!" Mom calls over her shoulder. "It's time to go."

The moment shatters like a dropped candy cane. Evan and I look at each other for a long second.

"I wish I didn't have to go," I say softly. "I wish…" If only I could be the kind of person who doesn't care what people think, the kind who does what she wants. But I think that Rachel only exists in an alternate universe where everybody eats cupcakes for breakfast and nobody ever has to go to gym class.

"It's okay," Evan says, reaching out his finger to give my nose an affectionate tap. "Two weeks isn't that long."

I know he's right, but it still feels like I took our perfect airport good-bye and turned it on its ear. Literally.

I'm still shaking as my mom and I go through the security checkpoint. When we get to the gate, it's time to say yet another good-bye.

My mom pulls me into a hug and starts sobbing into my hair.

"Mom," I say meekly. I try to think of something comforting to say, but I always freeze up when people get really emotional. "Um, at least there aren't any sharks in Orlando, so you don't have to worry about me being a shark-attack victim, right?"

She lets out a little laugh and pulls away. "It's not even on the water," she says, wiping her eyes.

"Exactly. No sharks. So I'll be fine. Will *you* be okay?"

Mom nods as she keeps sniffling. "I'll have plenty to keep me busy with apartment hunting and all the new Ladybug Cleaners clients." She leans in and kisses the top of my head. "Don't worry about me. Just have fun with your dad."

I feel bad that Mom is going to be working her buttons off and looking for apartments for us while I'm on vacation, but I couldn't say no when my dad asked me to visit. Besides, it might be months before we actually sell our house, so I doubt Mom will find a new place without me.

"I love you," she adds. "You know, I was about your age when I went on my first trip away from home. I found out so much about myself that summer. The experience showed me what kind of person I could be."

Oh boy. Now Mom's really getting cheesy. "Okay. I should go." I give her one last hug. If we draw this out any longer, I'm going to start crying too.

When Mom finally lets me go, I can't help peering back the way we came, even though Evan must be halfway across the airport by now.

I should feel like I'm at the start of an adventure. I should be excited to finally be leaving home and seeing my dad. But I can't help wishing I could have one more minute in my regular life before I go.

Chapter 2

After I spend the first hour of the flight to Florida replaying the world's worst kiss over and over in my head—ugh!—I finally switch to worrying about meeting my dad's girlfriend. What if she's an evil stepmother type, complete with British accent and nasty dog? Or what if she's a crazy Elvis impersonator? I can't deal with my dad kissing someone who has bigger sideburns than he does. Really, I don't think I can deal with my dad kissing *anyone*. Period.

Mom's new boyfriend is my middle school principal, which was awkward at first, but at least I had an idea of the kind of person he was. Ellie is a total question mark.

I try to distract myself by thinking about all the places I can't wait to visit with Dad over the next two weeks. When I was little, my perfect Florida vacation involved both of my parents taking me to every possible Orlando theme park. It didn't factor in the fact that my parents would be legally separated or that I'd be flying there by myself. Even though it's not the exact trip I always imagined, I'm determined to make the best of it.

By the time we land, I'm so anxious and excited that my stomach feels like it's a big bowl of jiggly pudding. It doesn't help that my "unaccompanied minor" badge has made the flight attendants treat me like a toddler through-out the whole flight. I'm starting to wonder if I'm even capable of walking out of the plane on my own or if it's better if they put me in a stroller.

I'm seriously considering darting back to the plane and begging the pilot to take me home when I spot my dad waiting for me at the gate. All my nervousness melts away the instant I see him grinning back at me.

"Dad!" I squeal. Even though I saw him a couple of weeks ago, his quick visit didn't do much to cure my with-drawal. I drop my bag and launch myself into his arms.

"I'm so happy to see you, Rachel Roo," he says, squeez-ing me tight. Then he shows one of the flight attendants his pass and ID, like he's checking me out of the library.

"Where's Ellie?" I ask as Dad grabs my carry-on. After all those hours of worrying, I'm almost disappointed not to have met her yet. Maybe she's outside with her pack of evil dogs. They probably don't let you park those in the garage.

"She's waiting for us by the baggage claim," he says.

I practically count each step as we make our way there, part of me enjoying that for now I have my dad to myself, the other part of me anxious to get the Big Meeting over with. I notice, suddenly, that my dad looks a lot more put together than he usually does. Instead of faded khakis and a wrinkled polo shirt, his clothes look pressed and brand-new. I have a feeling this must be Ellie's influence.

"Wow, look. Palm trees!" I cry, spotting a cluster of them through the airport window.

My dad smiles. "I'm glad you're finally getting to see the world outside New England."

When we get to the baggage claim, my dad waves to a petite woman standing nearby. "Rachel," he says, "this is Ellie."

She looks head-to-toe fancy, from her perfectly bobbed hair to her flowy blouse and linen pants. My fashion-obsessed best friend, Marisol, would totally approve. I'm suddenly self-conscious about my faded T-shirt and wrinkled shorts. Why couldn't I have put on a dress or something?

Ellie rushes over, smiling like the sun. "I'm so glad to

meet you!" she says with a slight southern accent as she furiously shakes my hand. Even her perfume smells expensive. I can tell right away why my dad likes her. She's as bubbly and friendly as he is. No sideburns or demon dogs. I feel myself relaxing as she beams at me.

Then Ellie turns and waves to a skinny boy who's about twelve, with a mop of hair hanging in his eyes and an iPad clutched in his hands.

"And this is my son, Caleb," Ellie says.

My mouth flops open. What the Shrek? Ellie has a *son*?

Caleb does a one-shoulder shrug-wave without actually looking up from his tablet. I guess I would think it was rude if I wasn't also being totally rude from shock. I look at my dad, but he's grinning back at me like everything is normal. Did he purposely not tell me about Caleb, or did he forget to mention him? Dad can be pretty scatterbrained sometimes, but this is big even for him.

"Hey," I finally manage to choke out.

Caleb shrugs again and starts frantically clicking something on his screen. I assume he's playing a game, although I can't tell what kind.

"Now," says Ellie, clapping her hands. Considering how

many rings she's wearing, I can't help wondering if it hurts. "Let's get you all settled at my place."

"Your place?" I say as we start walking toward the exit. "I thought I was staying at my dad's apartment."

"Not anymore!" Ellie chirps over her shoulder. "I told your father there was no way I'd let you sleep in that tiny box on my watch!"

"It's not *that* bad—" Dad breaks in, but Ellie keeps going.

"The resort is next door to where Caleb and I live, so you'll be able to relax there while your father and I are at work."

"Rachel, anything you want to say to Ellie?" my dad asks softly.

"Thank you, Ellie," I say, embarrassed that he had to pull it out of me. The thing is, I'd been hoping to finally spend some real time with my dad. How is that going to happen if I'm not even staying with him?

Ellie smiles. "No need to thank me. It's my pleasure. Once we get you settled in, we'll show you the resort. There are pools and tennis courts and spas—anything you could ever need."

Behind me, Caleb mutters something under his breath, not looking up from his iPad.

"What was that?" Ellie says. "Speak up, sweetheart! And get that hair out of your eyes."

"I said," Caleb mumbles, not touching his hair, "does 'anything you could ever need' include a sinkhole?"

I stop walking. "A sinkhole? As in, the ground disappears and stuff falls into it? Doesn't that only happen in disaster movies?"

"Oh, Caleb is being dramatic," Ellie says. "Yes, there was an *incident* at the resort last year, but it was only a tiny hole, and no one was hurt. They assure us it's perfectly safe now."

"Business has been a little slow to pick up since then," Dad says. "Still, they hired me to do scuba-diving tours for them, so it can't be that bad."

I manage a weak smile as we start walking again. We've only been in Florida for a few minutes, and already this trip has been full of surprises.

"I'm so glad you're here!" Ellie says suddenly, squeezing my arm. "Teddy has been buzzing about your visit all week!"

I blink. No one calls my dad Teddy. Most people call him Edward or Ted. But I guess if he doesn't mind, then why should I?

Dad gives me a grin as Ellie drapes her arm around my shoulder. Normally, I'd be totally uncomfortable about a stranger—my dad's girlfriend, no less!—being so touchy-feely with me, but Ellie seems so genuinely excited that I'm actually okay with it. Besides, how can I be unhappy when I'm finally with Dad again? Before he left, he and I shared everything. Now I only get to talk to him on the phone once a week, and I feel like all I've been doing is hiding the crazy stuff going on in my life. I can't wait for us to go back to how we used to be.

"Dad," I say as we pile into an elevator, "how do you do scuba diving when we're so far from the ocean?"

He shakes his head. "You'd be surprised how many folks think this whole state is on the beach. That's why we do half-day and all-day trips. We pack up passengers in a van and drive a couple hours to the coast, do some diving and snorkeling out there, and then drive back."

"Sounds like a long day for *you*," I say.

"It can be, but I promise I'll make time for you." Dad glances over at Ellie and smiles. "For all of you."

The way he looks at her makes something shift inside me. Like a sinkhole opening up in my chest.

"So when are we going to Disney?" I ask. "I can't wait to

stand on top of the Epcot shiny golf-ball building! I know they probably don't actually let you go up there, but maybe we could—"

"Whoa!" Dad says. "Let's leave the planning for later. For now, let's get you settled in."

When we leave the airport and step outside, a wall of heat slaps me in the face. For a second, I can't breathe. It's not hot. It's *steamy*. Like when I open the oven after it's done preheating. My T-shirt instantly feels plastered to my skin.

I'm actually panting by the time we get to the other side of the parking lot. No one else seems to even notice the suffocating heat. I guess they're used to it. Maybe my mom was right about Florida in the summertime.

We pile into Ellie's gleaming SUV while my dad loads my bags in the back. Caleb winds up sitting next to me, which is beyond awkward since he doesn't say a word the whole time. Every once in a while he glances up from his iPad and shoots a look in my direction, like he's trying to decide if I'm friend or foe.

Meanwhile, Ellie tells me about her job at the resort. She certainly likes to talk. "I used to be a nurse, back in the day. But after the divorce, I needed a change of pace, so I moved to Orlando and got a job answering phones at the Four Palms Resort. That didn't last long! I bounced around from job to job at the resort until they found one for me that was a good fit. Now, I'm the staffing manager. When we're looking to hire someone, people come to me. That's how I met your father, Rachel."

She gives me a sparkling smile in the rearview mirror. "Our scuba instructor had just quit after all the bad press from the sinkhole incident, and I was looking for someone to take his place. I signed up for one of your dad's trips, and the minute I met him, I knew he'd be perfect for the resort. It took a little while to convince my boss to hire him—"

"He was worried about my lack of experience," Dad explains.

"But Mark finally saw what I see in your father, that he's amazing!"

I can't decide if I should be happy or embarrassed to hear her saying things like that about my dad. It doesn't help that I have her son glaring at me from mere inches away. How can someone as bubbly as Ellie have a son as grumpy as Caleb? I try to focus on the scenery zipping past—hotel, hotel, Waffle House, hotel—but it's not much to look at.

I send Evan a message telling him I've arrived in

one piece. I blush as I think about the ear kiss again. Hopefully next time he tries to kiss me, I'll be able to keep ears, elbows, knees, and other nonessential body parts where they're supposed to be. That is, *if* he even tries to kiss me again.

I shake the thought out of my head as the car slows down and Ellie announces: "There's the resort. Isn't it a beauty?"

My first glimpse of Four Palms Resort and Spa actually makes me gasp. It's like something out of a movie. Clusters of palm trees, sparkling white buildings, and cascading fountains.

Who cares about extreme humidity, sinkholes, and unfriendly boys? I have officially arrived in heaven.

Chapter 3

Ellie's apartment is as nice as her clothes and her car. It's sleek and bright and museum-like. I can only imagine that Caleb's room is a dark cave compared to the rest of the place.

"This is amazing!" I say when Ellie shows me the guest room where I'll be staying. It has a giant bed, its own bathroom, and—the kicker—a balcony that overlooks the Four Palms Resort next door. I have a feeling I'll be hanging out there for hours (with a very cold lemonade in my hand so I don't pass out from the heat). Even though it's early evening, the air is still hot and sticky.

"You'll be sharing this balcony with Caleb," Ellie says as we go to check it out. "His room is right next door."

"Most of the other apartments here have balconies way bigger than this," Caleb mutters. "They should have designed it so that all of them were the same size."

Ellie pats him on the shoulder. "Caleb is interested in architecture, just like his father. Aren't you? Tuck in your shirt, dear. It looks sloppy."

Caleb just grunts and keeps tapping away on his iPad. These two certainly have a weird relationship.

I glance at my dad to see how he's dealing with Caleb's "cheery" mood, but he's grinning at us like everything is perfect.

"What are those tents for?" I ask, spotting a couple of brightly colored canopies set up inside the resort.

Ellie smiles. "They're for a little event we're putting together next week, a mini Renaissance festival. We thought it might help to bring in some business."

"Wow, does that mean you'll have jousting and stuff?" I ask, remembering a festival my dad took me to when I was little.

"Jousters, musicians, jugglers—you name it!"

"And catapults," Caleb chimes in. For once he actually looks up from his tablet. I realize that his eyes are the exact same shade of gray as Ellie's. "There's a design-your-own-catapult competition for kids," he goes on, his face suddenly full of excitement. "I'm going to win it."

"Now, let's not brag, dear," Ellie says.

But Caleb is already back to tapping on the screen.

"Ellie, why don't we let Rachel settle in and then we can go get some dinner at the resort," Dad says.

"Oh," I say. "I was hoping we could go to one of the restaurants at Downtown Disney tonight. Remember, Dad? We always talked about checking it out. It's free to get in."

Dad opens his mouth to answer, but Ellie jumps in. "But it's Sunday. We always eat at the resort on Sundays. Don't we, Teddy?"

My dad nods and gives me an apologetic smile. "Ellie's big on traditions."

"They make families strong!" she chirps.

I can't help feeling disappointed, but I have to remind myself that it's only my first night here. It won't kill me to wait a day to dive into all the stuff on my list.

We all start to go back into the room, but suddenly Ellie reaches out and grabs my arm. "Stay out here with me a minute," she whispers.

I stare at her in confusion. Do I have something in my teeth and she's too embarrassed to tell me in front of the others?

When Dad and Caleb are inside, she pulls me over to the

corner of the balcony and says in a loud whisper, "I wanted to tell you how much your father means to me, Rachel. He's the best thing to happen to me in a long time."

"Oh. Good," I say. My cheeks are already flushed from the heat, but they're suddenly even hotter.

"I can't wait to marry him," she says, her eyes shining.

My jaw drops. *Marry* him? Is she saying that she and my dad are *engaged*?

"But shhh," she adds. "Don't say anything to your dad, okay? I want it to be a huge surprise when I pop the question."

Before I can stammer out an answer, my dad calls from inside: "Rachel? Ellie? What are you two doing out there?"

"Just some girl talk!" Ellie calls back, giving me a big wink. Then she squeezes my shoulder and hurries indoors.

I'm in a daze as I stumble back into the frostily air-conditioned room. Caleb's already disappeared and Dad is lugging my bags into the corner.

"Roo? Are you all right?" he asks when he sees what must be a stony look on my face.

Am I all right? I have no idea what to make of what Ellie told me. Part of me hopes I hallucinated the whole thing. Heat makes people do that sometimes, doesn't it?

"Yeah," I say, forcing myself to smile. "Just tired."

He pulls me into a quick hug. "I'm so glad you're here, Roo. You have no idea how much I've missed you." A pained expression flashes across his face, like having me here actually makes him sad for some reason.

"I've missed you too," I say.

"We'll let you relax for a little while, and then we'll get some dinner. Okay?"

I nod as he leaves the room. Then I stand there, still dazed, replaying what Ellie said. My parents aren't even divorced yet. How could my dad get engaged again? And when Ellie said she's going to "pop the question," did she mean sometime in the far-off future or did she mean tomorrow? Oh my goldfish. What if she does it while I'm here? Even if she seems nice, how am I supposed to be okay with that? It's totally bizarre!

But I guess if they're happy...

Are they happy? Ellie certainly seems that way, but Dad? He was smiling a lot, but now that I think about it, he hasn't laughed once since I got here. That doesn't seem like the dad I know at all.

Chapter 4

When I finish unpacking, I venture out of my room to find Ellie sitting on the couch reading some kind of medical textbook. It's not exactly the type of light reading I'd picture her doing. In fact, most of her shelves are full of books on nursing and medicine. It's strange to think Ellie had a totally different life before she started working at the resort.

"Are you hungry?" she asks.

"I guess so." The truth is, my stomach is in knots from everything that's happened today. I'm not sure I could get it to unclamp for anything, not even a slice of chocolate peanut butter pie.

"Great, let's go meet your dad." She gets to her feet and grabs her purse. "Caleb, we're going!"

A minute later, his door creaks open. "Do I have to?" he asks.

"Families that eat together stay together," she says. Wow, Ellie really likes all those cheesy family sayings. Weirdly, it sounds like she believes they're true.

Caleb lets out a long sigh, tucks his iPad under his arm, and comes to join us.

The instant we leave Ellie's apartment and start walking over to the resort, I'm sweating like crazy. How does no one else notice that it's a bajillion degrees here? If I don't get used to it soon, I might have to start keeping ice packs in my pockets.

My dad is waiting for us outside one of the dozen restaurants in the resort. He gives Ellie a kiss on the cheek as if he didn't just see her an hour ago and then we head inside.

I'm excited to catch up with my dad over dinner, but Ellie keeps chattering the whole time. Dad smiles as he nods along, but he never laughs. I don't get it. Does he actually like Ellie, or is he just humoring her?

Finally, when Ellie gets up to use the bathroom, I see my chance to talk to my dad. But when I open my mouth to say something, only air comes out. What is going on? My dad and I always have tons to talk about. I guess so much has happened since he left home that I don't even know where to start.

"Hey, Dad, I have joke for you," I finally say. If there's one thing he and I have in common, it's our sense of humor. "Why can't a bicycle stand on its own?"

He blinks at me for a second. "Why?"

"Because it's two tired!" I say, erupting into giggles.

Caleb lets out a "wah-wah" sound like a trombone, but I expect Dad to laugh. Instead, he looks distracted, like he barely even heard what I said. My laughter fades as I focus on buttering my roll.

"So, Rachel," Dad says after a long silence, "are you excited about starting high school?" It's the kind of question a stranger would ask.

I shrug. "Marisol is. She keeps talking about wanting to start a fashion club. I'm hoping they'll have a baking club or something."

"Will you girls be in the same classes?" he asks.

"We won't know until orientation in a couple of weeks."

Dad sighs. "I'm sorry I won't be there."

I realize, suddenly, that for the first time ever, Dad will miss my first day of school. Normally, he puts a funny limerick or a puzzle in my lunch. But this year...nothing. Is that why he's acting so weird? Because he's realizing how much stuff he's missed since he's been gone?

Before I can figure out a way to ask him, Ellie scampers back from the bathroom. As she spreads her napkin on her lap, she turns to me and says, "Rachel, I wanted to talk to you."

I put down my roll. Oh no. Is she going to announce something even bigger than the getting married thing? I don't even know what that would be. That she and my dad are going to be on the first manned mission to Mars?

"I have a bit of a problem on my hands," she continues. "An employee at the café here was let go this week, and I've been desperately trying to find a replacement. Another girl, Ava, was supposed to start working tomorrow, but she changed her mind at the last minute. That means the café is sorely understaffed. So I was thinking that you might be able to help out in the café until I find a replacement."

I stare at her. At least she's not talking about marriage or interplanetary travel, but I have no idea how to react to this news, either.

"I know it's not exactly the vacation you had in mind," Dad jumps in, flashing me an apologetic smile. "But it would probably only be for a couple of days. After that, you'll be free to enjoy yourself however you want. And I should be able to get a few days off to spend with you."

"But what about the fun stuff we had planned?" A huge part of the reason I came down here was so that Dad and I could finally do our dream trip together. And now I'm supposed to spend part of it working?

"We'll still do lots of things together," Dad says. "I promise. But remember that I'll be at work too."

I play with my napkin for a minute. It's definitely not the way I saw my trip going. "Can't you find someone else?" I ask Ellie.

The hope on her face evaporates. "I suppose I'll have to." She sighs. "Oh well. It was worth a try!"

She goes back to studying her menu like the discussion is over, but when I glance over at Dad, I see how disappointed he is. Suddenly, I feel terrible. The last thing I want during this vacation is to let him down.

"Wait," I say softly. "Are you sure it'll only be a couple of days? Because if it is, then…I guess I'll do it."

Dad's whole face breaks out into a smile. "That's my girl!"

"This means so much to me," Ellie says, beaming. "The tips at the café are great, so you'll have some extra spending money right away."

I do like the sound of that, but I can't help returning

their big smiles with one that feels painfully fake. When I glance at Caleb, he has a smug look on his face like he thinks I've just gotten suckered into something. Maybe he's right. All I know is that, so far, nothing about this trip has gone the way I planned.

Chapter 5

Ellie knocks on my door ridiculously early the next morning, waking me from nightmares about sinkholes opening up under my bed.

"Rise and shine, sleepy bear!" she says. "Since it's your first day, I want to introduce you to everyone at the café."

I try not to let out a bearlike growl as I stumble into the shower. I was up late last night talking to Marisol, telling her about all the disastrous stuff that happened yesterday, from the almost-kiss to the almost-stepmom to the almost-job. Marisol clucked at all the right places and reminded me that I only have to survive here for two weeks. Right now it feels more like two million.

While I shampoo my hair, my stomach starts fluttering like crazy. I've never been great at talking to strangers, and today I not only have to work with people I don't know, but I have to help customers. Why did I ever agree to do this? I'm good with food, not with people!

When I'm finally dressed and ready to go, I follow Ellie out the door. "I can't thank you enough for helping me out, Rachel," she says as she leads me toward the resort. "I think you'll like the other girls. They're about your age."

I almost laugh. Clearly, Ellie doesn't know much about me if she thinks I'm going to have an easy time making friends.

"Over there is the spa," Ellie says, pointing at one of the buildings. "Whenever I'm looking a little haggard, I stop in there. Let me know if you'd like me to make you an appointment sometime."

"Oh…thanks," I say, wondering if that means I'm looking "haggard." I'm sure I at least look like a rat drowning in its own sweat. How can it be so hot already when it's barely past dawn?

As we weave through the resort, Ellie waves and says hello to everyone we pass, like she's on a parade float. She also knows the names of every employee we see, and she asks them about their spouses or kids or pets. No wonder the resort put her in charge of hiring.

"There's Mark," Ellie says as an older man in a gray suit comes out of the main building. "He's the resort manager and my boss." She drags me over so we can say hello.

"It's nice to meet you," Mark says, giving me a firm handshake. "Your father's been a great asset here the past few weeks. I'm sure we'll enjoy having you work for us too."

"Thanks. You too," I blurt out. Ugh. Why can't I say something normal to a stranger for once in my life?

Luckily, Mark doesn't seem to notice my total awkwardness. Instead, he smiles at me and then turns to Ellie and says, "I have to be off. Someone reported one of the guests practicing fire breathing near the tennis courts. This Renaissance festival was a great idea, Ellie, but I have to admit that I'll be glad when it's over." He chuckles and hurries away.

"Isn't Mark the best?" Ellie says. "If it weren't for him, I don't think I'd still be working here. Any other place would have gotten fed up with me changing jobs all the time, but Mark's been great about giving me a second chance. And a third, and a fourth!"

A minute later, we round a corner and come to a café right across from a hair salon. "Four Palms Café" the sign says in black-and-pink letters. When we go inside, I'm smacked in the face by the smell of stale coffee and greasy pastries. The place is empty except for a couple of middle-aged men in business suits sipping iced lattes in the corner.

Behind the counter, two girls in black aprons with pink frills are bustling around prepping for the day. Ellie introduces the blond older girl as Carrie, the manager of the café, and the tall girl with the perfect tan as Taylor. Then she tells them that I'll be helping out for the next few days until she can hire someone long-term.

The girls barely glance up while Ellie's talking. Even though the place is empty, it seems like they're expecting a mad rush at any second.

"Now, girls," says Ellie, her voice even higher and bubblier than normal. "Remember what we talked about. After the, er, incident, it was natural for things to lag a bit, but we can't let that get us down. There has to be a way to get this place swinging again!"

"Yes, ma'am," Carrie says in a way that makes me wonder if she's being sarcastic.

Ellie turns back to me. "If you have any problems, I'm at extension three-five-three." Then she's gone, and I'm left alone with two girls who seem not to care that I'm standing here.

Finally, Carrie comes around the counter, eyeing me up and down. "So you're Ava?" she says finally.

"Uh—"

"Thank goodness you're here," Taylor calls over the counter.

"Yeah, ever since Melody got fired, it's been crazy," Carrie says. "Anyway, follow me. I'll show you how to make the croissants."

"I already know how to make croissants," I say.

Carrie shakes her head. "They're really particular about how we do stuff here."

I follow her to the ovens in the back. Luckily, the air-conditioning is cranking at full blast or I'd never survive. As Carrie chatters on about the pastries and sandwiches the café serves and Taylor rushes around filling coffee urns, I try to take everything in.

It looks like the café doesn't make anything from scratch. Their pastries are all the premade kind you just pop in the oven, and even their sandwich fillings come prepackaged. Gross.

"Mostly we'll be having you make the food, but sometimes you might need to jump on a register or help a customer." Carrie turns to me. "You know how to do all that, don't you?"

I blink at her.

"So, Ava, do you have any questions?"

I know I should correct her, but I'm totally overwhelmed. At least the food part will be easy, but handling customers? And a cash register? And counting money? I've never done any of those things!

Before I can confess how totally clueless I am, Carrie laughs and says, "That's what I like to hear. Melody was always asking way too many questions. It drove me nuts. Okay, let's get ready before the breakfast crowd comes." She shoves an apron in my hands and rushes off.

All I can do is follow.

Chapter 6

After I shadow Carrie for a little while, I start to get the hang of things. I mostly have to put the pastries in the oven and take them out again when the timer goes off. Any robot with oven mitts could do this job.

I taste a cooling croissant and cringe. It's not awful, but there's a suspicious aftertaste to it, almost like black pepper.

"Disgusting, right?" Taylor says, seeing my face. "We're pretty sure all the stuff here is made at a spice factory. The resort must get it at a really good price."

Carrie snorts. "Too bad no one actually wants to eat donuts that taste like"—she takes a bite—"basil."

I'm tempted to ask why we can't make the pastries from scratch, but I don't want to rock the boat, not when I'm only going to be here for a couple of days.

At around 8 a.m., the breakfast rush starts. Some of the people who bustle into the café are clearly tourists who are staying at the hotel (based on their golf clothes and flip-flops), but most of the customers are resort employees who are there for their morning iced-coffee fix. Pretty soon I'm so busy that I don't even have time to stress about being surrounded by complete strangers. I'm relieved not to have to touch the cash registers, though. Knowing me, I'd probably accidentally start handing out Monopoly money.

Once the last customer leaves, I'm surprised that most of our pastries are untouched.

"Yeah, we mostly just sell coffee," Carrie says when I ask her about it. "I keep telling Mark that if we had food people actually wanted to eat, we wouldn't be losing so much money, but he thinks I'm just complaining."

"So I have to make all these gross pastries every day even though we know people won't buy them?" I ask.

"Yup," she says. "The lunch rush is a little better but still not great. You'd think the fact that the café is on the verge of having to shut down would make them change the way they do things here, but they're so set in their ways that they don't want to admit anything is wrong."

If the café has been serving these weirdly spicy pastries for a while, I'm amazed they're still open at all.

"So, Ava," Taylor says, turning to me. "Someone said

you just moved here from Texas and that you're into riding horses." She positions herself with one hand on the counter and does some balletlike moves. I'm surprised by how graceful she is.

"Oh, um, no. I'm from Massachusetts."

"Ha!" says Carrie. "See, Taylor? I told you my brother was making things up to mess with you. And you always believe him."

"No, I don't!" Taylor says. I can tell by the way she's blushing that she has a crush on Carrie's brother, whether she's willing to admit it or not. She turns back to me. "At least tell me the horseback riding part is true!"

I blink. She looks like she really wants it to be true, but I can't flat-out lie. "I do like horses," I say slowly. "But—"

"See?" Taylor flashes Carrie a triumphant grin before I can admit that I'd be too terrified to ever even touch a horse. "Kai was telling the truth about something."

"Maybe this time," Carrie says, "but he's always trying to push people's buttons." She glances at me and explains, "Taylor moved here at the start of the summer so she hasn't realized that my brother is a total freak yet."

Taylor sighs. "My dad's been having a hard time finding a job, so we've been moving around a lot. We were in Miami at my aunt's place for a while, but now we're here." She does a little twirl that makes her look like a dancing doll.

"Taylor does ballet," Carrie says. "Isn't she good?'

I groan inwardly. How am I supposed to tell them the truth when Carrie and Taylor keep switching topics so fast that I can barely keep up?

Taylor stops midspin. "*Used* to do ballet," she says. "We can't really afford it anymore." She goes off to restock the napkin dispensers, her shoulders stooped.

"So, um, about the horseback riding…" I start to say.

Carrie waves her hand. "I'm not the person to talk to about that. I hate anything with fur. Except for my brother." She lets out a snort-laugh, which I'm starting to suspect is her trademark. "You'll probably see Kai later. He works at the smoothie stand by the pool." She glances at Taylor who still has a far-off look on her face.

I sigh. Forget it. I'm only working here a couple of days. Who cares if these girls think I'm someone else? Besides, how often do I get a chance to hang out with older kids and actually fit in?

"Is Taylor okay?" I say instead.

Carrie shrugs. "It was stupid of me to bring up ballet.

Now that her dad can't afford to pay for classes, she gets really bummed talking about it," she says. Then her face brightens and she calls out, "Okay, guys, it's game time."

"What does that mean?" I ask.

"When it's dead in here, we take turns making up games. Yesterday we played Catch the Danish, so we need something new today."

"Hmmm." Taylor comes over to the counter, rubbing her chin like she's stroking an invisible beard. Her mood is a million times lighter than it was a minute ago. "It's my turn today, so how about, in honor of Ava…" She picks up a wooden spoon and a donut. "Horseshoes?"

"I think you mean Horse Donuts," Carrie says, laughing. She grabs the spoon and goes to set it up in the middle of the floor.

"Do you own any horses?" Taylor asks me as she picks out some of the stalest donuts to toss.

"Oh, um. Yeah. Two of them," I blurt out.

Taylor lets out an impressed whistle. "You guys must have a lot of money. Horses are expensive."

They are? The closest I've ever been to a horse is on a carousel. "Oh no, we don't. We, um, adopted them. From an animal shelter. They were free. We adopted a couple of cats there too. They all live in the barn. Next to the duck pond."

Whoa. Now I have two horses, some cats, and enough ducks to warrant an entire *pond*?

Luckily, before I add that I also own a snow leopard, Carrie announces that I have to go first in Horse Donuts.

"I don't think so," I say. Hand-eye coordination has never been my thing.

"Come on!" says Carrie. "Have a little fun. Otherwise this job will bore you to death. Trust me, this is my third summer working here. Even before the sinkhole killed our business, it was still really boring most of the time."

Wow, that means Carrie must be at least seventeen. I don't think I've ever had an actual conversation with an upperclassman before.

"Okay," I say. After all, I'm hanging out with older girls and managing to blend in. I don't want them thinking I'm a wuss.

I stand by the counter, take a deep breath, and toss the first donut. It sails right past the spoon and bounces off one of the tables.

Carrie and Taylor burst out laughing. I get into throwing stance again, wiggling my butt like I've seen Red Sox players do, which only makes the other girls laugh harder. I can't help grinning. Usually, Marisol is the only one who gets my goofiness. Well, and my dad, but he and I haven't been all that in tune recently.

I grab a powdered donut, wind up my arm, and let it go. It wobbles as it flies through the air before it hits one of the café windows, leaving a white imprint on the glass.

"Look, Ava, it's snowing!" Carrie says.

We're all giggling as I wind up again, but before I can throw my final donut, the door to the café swings open and Caleb shuffles in.

Chapter 7

Caleb's eyes laser into me and then go to the donut in my hand and the spoon on the floor. "What are you doing?" he asks.

"Nothing," I say, shoving the donut into my apron pocket. I can practically hear Carrie and Taylor listening to our conversation as they go pick up the tossed donuts. "What are *you* doing here?"

"I have to come to the resort after soccer camp every day until my mom's done with work. Can I get a cookie?" He points at a chocolate chip one in the display case.

"Are you sure? They taste like curry."

He shrugs. "I don't care. I'm hungry."

As I wrap the cookie in some thin paper, I expect Carrie to ring it up, but she just waves her hand and says, "No charge." I guess she knows he's Ellie's son.

I give Caleb a weak smile as I hand him the cookie.

What if the other girls call me "Ava" or start talking about me riding horses? Or what if he calls me "Rachel" in front of them?

Since I'm praying for him to leave, of course, Caleb picks this moment to suddenly get chatty. "Have you seen the people on stilts walking around? They're going to be in the festival."

I shake my head.

He chuckles. "They keep falling over."

"That's because they don't know what they're doing," Carrie says. "My brother's one of them. Your mom asked him to do it, even though he's not trained or anything."

Caleb shrugs. "Yeah, Mom likes to do stuff like that. Are you guys going to be in the festival?"

"I'm supposed to sell cotton candy," Carrie says.

"I'm one of the dancers," Taylor pipes up. "It should be fun."

"Do you know who's judging the catapult competition?" he asks.

Both girls shake their heads, making Caleb sigh. "Okay. I should go." Then he heads for the door, already looking at his iPad again.

As the door swings shut behind him, I let out a sigh of

relief that he didn't accidentally give me away. How do I always get myself into these situations?

"How do you know The Spy?" Carrie says, watching through the window as Caleb disappears around the corner.

"The Spy?" I say.

Carrie rolls her eyes. "Ellie sends him in here to spy on us every couple of days."

I must look worried because Taylor says, "We don't think he actually tells her anything. How do you know him?"

"Um, Ellie introduced us this morning. He seems kind of bratty."

"He's actually not that bad," Carrie says.

"Besides," Taylor adds, "his family is pretty crazy, so you can't blame him for being a pain."

"Oh, Ava," Carrie says. "I think Taylor, Kai, and I are going mini-golfing tonight. You want to come?"

It takes me a second to realize she's talking to me. "Tonight?"

"You can see Carrie's new car," says Taylor. "She just got it a couple weeks ago and wouldn't stop talking about it for days."

Whoa. Carrie has a car? I've never been friends with some-one with a car. I've never even been friends with someone who was old enough to drive!

"I—I wish I could," I say, and I really mean it. How much fun would it be to drive around with a bunch of older kids? But, of course, I can't. "Sorry, I have plans later."

"Maybe tomorrow," Carrie says. "Ugh, my hair is such a mess today." She flips her head down and runs her hands through her glossy hair before snapping it back. Somehow that simple move makes her blond waves look even better than they did a second ago.

Taylor puts her arm around my shoulders. "You're so much more fun than Melody."

"Wh—what happened to her?" I ask. "Why did she get fired?"

Taylor's smile fades. "She was caught stealing from the register."

"Yeah, heads up about that," says Carrie. "They're pretty lenient about a lot of stuff here, but stealing isn't one of them. So watch out, okay?"

"Oh, don't worry," I say. Not only did I learn my lesson about stealing after I "borrowed" almost three hundred dollars from my college fund, but my dad would never forgive me if I got into trouble while I was here visiting him.

"Melody also lied about stuff all the time," Taylor says.

"Trying to make herself sound a lot more interesting than she actually was."

"To be honest," Carrie says, "we couldn't stand her. You're definitely an upgrade, Ava."

I swallow. I know I just met these girls, but already I like them. I don't want them to hate me for lying to them like they hated Melody. So I bite my lip and try not to look like a big, fat liar.

"There was one good thing about Melody, though," Taylor says. She digs around under the counter and pulls out a fancy old copy of one of the Nancy Drew books.

"She read mysteries?" I say.

"She put some really funny stuff in the Gossip File," Carrie says. "Check it out."

As I take the book from Taylor, I realize that it's thicker than it should be. Tucked in between the pages of the novel are dozens of pieces of hotel stationery covered in different handwriting.

"What are all these notes?" I say.

"Gossip about the resort," Carrie says. "Everyone has to add a few things when they start working here. And guess what, Ava? You're next!"

"What?"

"Normally you'd have to add ten interesting pieces of gossip," Taylor says. "That's how many I had to do. But since you just started, we can go easy on you."

"Yup," says Carrie. "You only have to do five." She hands me a notepad of hotel stationery. "Once you write them on there, we'll add them to the file."

"But…but what am I supposed to write?" I say.

"Anything juicy," says Carrie. "You can take the Gossip File home with you tonight and look through it for ideas, but make sure no one sees it. Especially Ellie. That woman has it in for us."

"What do you mean?" I ask.

"She's always trying to get us to do extra work so she can kiss up to Mark and show him how perfect she is." Carrie rolls her eyes. "Like this Renaissance festival thing. It was her idea, but now she wants us to dress up and put tons of work into it while she takes the credit. I bet if Ellie had her way, she'd fire us and put little robots in our places."

Taylor laughs and starts doing jerky robot movements while I try not to look guilty. I feel like I should stand up for Ellie. I haven't known her for very long, but she seems to really care about this resort and everyone in it. Then again, admitting that Ellie is dating my dad would be like saying that I'm the boss's daughter. I don't want the other girls feeling awkward around me because of that.

I start to flip through the Gossip File, but Carrie pulls the book out of my hands. "Better hide this for now," she says, tucking it back under the counter, behind a couple of napkin dispensers. "You can get it later."

"So, Ava, do you have a boyfriend?" Taylor asks. My face must go bright red because she lets out a squeal. "What's his name?"

"Evan," I say. "We…we just became official."

"Tell us everything!" says Taylor, leaning back in one of the chairs.

As I start describing Evan in all his cuteness, I stop worrying about telling the other girls my real identity. Being Ava feels different—better—than being Rachel. Rachel doesn't hang out with older girls and talk about her boyfriend. I bet Ava wouldn't have been freaked out about kissing her boyfriend good-bye at the airport. And Ava definitely wouldn't feel awkward around her dad and his girlfriend.

Maybe living as Ava for a couple of days is exactly what I need, like a little vacation from being me.

Chapter 8

After work, I decide it's time I take advantage of being in Florida and actually go swimming. I change into my bathing suit at Ellie's and then, armed with sunglasses and reading material, head back to the resort to hang out by one of the four interconnected pools. The humidity is so bad that I'm practically wheezing by the time I find a recliner in the shade.

I'm surprised by how empty the pool is, considering the heat. Wouldn't everyone want to be swimming?

The instant I take my flip-flops off, my feet start burning on the concrete.

"Ouch!" I cry as I prance toward the pool. When I dive in, the water is nice and warm. Well, maybe a little more than that. It's like bathwater, which, I have to admit, isn't all that refreshing in the crazy heat. I dunk my head under, hoping it'll cool me down, but when I come up for a breath, I can barely feel where the water ends and the air begins. Who knew air could feel so wet?

I halfheartedly tread water for a minute before climbing out of the almost-hot pool. So much for that idea. If only Dad were here, he'd find a way to make this fun. Last time we went to the beach, he spent part of the day wearing my pink sunglasses just to make me laugh.

I settle into a recliner and grab a memoir by the creator of *Pastry Wars*, my favorite cooking show, but I only get about three pages in before my sweat starts dripping onto the paper. Ew.

Defeated, I get my stuff together and head toward Ellie's. On the way, I hear a horrible screeching sound coming from behind one of the buildings. When I peer around the side, I spot a handful of resort employees playing violins and flutes and other instruments. It takes me a minute to realize that they're butchering the kind of jaunty tune you'd expect to hear at a Renaissance festival. I wonder if this is how the Pied Piper got all those rats to jump into the river. Maybe he played so badly that the rodents were willing to do anything to make the torture end.

I quickly cover my ears and hurry away. When I get

back to Ellie's, I find Caleb in the kitchen making himself a sandwich.

"Aren't we going out for dinner in an hour?" I say.

He shakes his head. "Nope, it's Monday. Date night."

"Date night?" I ask blankly.

"My mom and Teddy always go out by themselves on Mondays. It's another of her dumb traditions."

"But…but they won't do that when I'm here, will they? I mean, I'm only in town for a couple of weeks."

Caleb shrugs. "Good luck convincing her of that," he says before heading back to his room.

I decide to ignore what he said and get ready for dinner. Dad wouldn't ditch me like that, would he? But when I come out all dressed and ready, sure enough, Dad and Ellie are just about to head out the door.

"Sorry, Roo," Dad says. "I forgot to tell you that Ellie and I have plans, but Caleb said he filled you in."

"There's some lasagna in the fridge for you," Ellie says. "We won't be out too late."

"But…"

"You'll be okay by yourself for an evening, right?" Dad asks.

I can't sound like a baby and say I won't be, but

I can't believe he would abandon me on my second night here!

"Yeah," I say weakly. "I'll watch *Pastry Wars* reruns or something."

"We'll make it up to you tomorrow, okay?" he says. "I'll take you to see my place. I promise."

As I watch them leave, I want to believe him, but Dad's promises are starting to feel a little hollow.

Since I've lost my appetite, I head back to my room and lock the door. Then I carefully take out the Gossip File, which I wrapped in napkins and an old apron to smuggle into Ellie's apartment.

On the first page of notes, someone wrote: "The resort seems beautiful and perfect. It's oddly comforting to know that under its flawless exterior lurk many strange secrets." After that, the pages of notes are filled with different handwriting. Probably at least ten people have added gossip to the book. I wonder how long it's been around the café and who started it in the first place.

I flip through pages of tidbits about people I don't know. Some are disgusting: "Chandra lets little kids pee in the kiddie pool and pretends she doesn't see them." *Ick!* That one is dated three years ago, but I have *no* intention of even looking at the kiddie pool again. Some are funny: "Alan wears socks all the time because he has an extra toe on his right foot." And some are just bizarre: "Mark calls his wife every day to remind her to record his soap operas."

I'm pretty sure this last one is about Ellie's boss. I never would have pegged Mark for a soap opera fan. Whoever started the Gossip File was right. It *is* oddly reassuring to know that a place that seems so perfect is just as flawed as I am.

Some of the gossip is pretty bad, like people cheating on their spouses, but I skim over all of that. It feels wrong to read that kind of stuff about people I don't even know.

When I start mulling over the five things I have to write down, my mind goes blank. All I can think about is what I wrote about people in the Dirt Diary that I kept at the beginning of the summer. Collecting people's secrets made me feel so slimy that I definitely don't want to do it again, but I have to write something. Carrie and Taylor can't think I'm a total wimp. Not only do they not care that I'm younger than they are, but they're also really fun to hang out with.

Maybe the stuff I write doesn't have to be bad, I realize. The part about the extra toe was gross, but it wasn't anything awful. It was just the truth. If I write down things that are true, things that wouldn't hurt anyone if people found out about them, maybe that will be okay.

I scratch my head for a minute, grab a sheet of stationery, and then take out a pencil.

The food at the café tastes like a spice factory exploded on it. There, that's true. I suck on the pencil for a minute and then add a couple of quotes that I've heard people say about the food. This might not qualify as "juicy gossip," but it's a start.

Chapter 9

I wake up before my alarm goes off and lie in bed listening to the air conditioner going full blast and Caleb snoring through the wall. The longer I lie here, the worse I feel. I know I shouldn't complain. I mean, after all these years of dreaming about it, I'm finally in *Florida*! But this trip has been one big disappointment so far.

For some reason, I start thinking about what Mom said at the airport, that this trip might help me figure out who I am. So far, all it's shown me is that I'm a total pushover. I'd rather go along with people calling me by the wrong name than correct them, and I'd let my dad's girlfriend hog all his time instead of demanding that he spend it with me.

Well, it might be too late to tell everyone I'm not Ava, but I'm not giving up on my perfect vacation just yet. I have a little over a week and a half to reconnect with Dad and make our special Disney trip happen. That should be plenty of time.

As I get out of bed, I can't help smiling as I remember Evan's and my phone conversation last night when he told me how much he missed me. And then, for some reason, he had me talk to his guitar since he claimed it missed me too. At least our relationship is one thing in my life that's finally going right.

I'm about to head off to the café when there's a knock on my bedroom door. I find Caleb standing there with a shopping bag.

"My mom's already at work, but she wanted me to give you this," he mumbles, shoving the bag into my hand. Then he turns and stomps into the kitchen.

I dig around in the bag and pull out a yellow-and-white striped sundress. It's not exactly my style, but I could imagine Marisol loving it. I have no idea why Ellie is buying me clothes. Maybe now that she's upgraded my dad's wardrobe, she's started on me?

I tuck the Gossip File into a plastic bag so I can sneak it back to the café. Then I spread the dress out on my bed so I can try it on after work. There's no point in wearing it to the café where I'd just spill stuff all over it.

As I make my way through the resort, I pass a troupe of jugglers hanging out by the pool and a girl struggling to swing a sword that probably weighs about a hundred pounds more than she does. They all look pretty clueless and miserable.

Then I spot a man poised in front of a wooden target and pointing a bow and arrow in every direction except the right one. I quickly cover my head and flee. I don't stop running until I catch sight of Ellie on her hands and knees in front of a dead tree that's tucked away in the corner of the courtyard.

"Good morning!" she calls out when she sees me, waving me over with a watering can. "Have you met my tree yet?"

I stare at the pile of dried-out branches. "Is it, um, feeling okay?"

"It's a little under the weather right now."

It's not the only one, I think as I fan myself with my hand. I make sure to keep the Gossip File safely tucked under my arm, still wrapped in the plastic bag, so Ellie doesn't notice it.

"I planted this tree when I first started working here at Four Palms," she says, pouring some water near its base. "It was only a sapling then. And now look at it!"

I try not to grimace as I glance at it since Ellie clearly wants me to look impressed.

"One day, it's going to grow oranges," she says.

I figure it's best not to point out that I'm not even sure we're looking at an orange tree. Instead, I can't help asking, "How was date night with my dad?" I don't even bother hiding the bitterness in my voice.

She lets out a soft giggle. "It was lovely! Tonight is pizza night at my place, though, so that will be fun for all of us. Make sure to wear your new dress!"

"Oh yeah, thanks for the dress," I say. "It's cute." I don't mention that I'm not sure it's really my style. "So we're going to your place tonight? What about having dinner at Disney?"

"You'll need to talk to your dad about that. He's in charge of the plans while you're here."

Obviously, that's not true. Ellie is definitely the one calling the shots.

"Is my dad okay?" I can't help asking.

Ellie looks at me in surprise. "Last time I talked to him he seemed fine. Why?"

"He just hasn't been acting like himself. Dad usually jokes around all the time and he's always laughing, but ever since I've been here, he's seemed different."

"Really?" Ellie wrinkles her forehead. "I guess he has been a little busy at work, but he seems like his normal self to me!"

"Maybe I need to spend more time with him, just me and him," I say, hoping Ellie gets the hint. She doesn't.

"You'll have plenty of time to see him tonight," she says. "Pizza night is always fun. Even Caleb gets into it." She sighs. "Ever since the divorce, he's been so different. If he's not playing with that tablet of his, all he talks about is being with his dad."

"Where does his dad live?" I ask.

"Not too far from here. But he's in Arizona on a building project right now. That's why Caleb is staying with me."

"Oh...I thought he lived with you."

She shakes her head. "No, no. He had a choice during the divorce, and he chose to stay with his father. I keep trying to convince him to change his mind, but no luck so far."

Even though she's smiling, I can tell how hurt she is. I might still be annoyed with her, but I also feel a little bad for her. "When my parents split up," I find myself saying, "I thought I wanted to go with my dad. But now

I'm glad I stayed with my mom. Maybe he needs time to realize that."

She reaches out and squeezes my elbow. "You're right. Maybe one day he can be as mature about the situation as you are, Rachel."

I blush at the compliment. It's nice to be called mature for once. Ellie is a little intense, but maybe she's not so bad.

Before I get to the café, I grab a pencil and the pad of hotel stationery from my pocket. I hesitate for a second, not sure if I should write down what I just found out. I'm not even sure it's good enough info for the Gossip File, but it's the best I have, so I grip the pencil tightly and write, "Ellie's son doesn't live with her. He chose to live with his dad after the divorce."

As I tuck the notes back into my pocket, I wonder if Caleb and his dad are as close as my dad and I are. Or *were*. Until this trip, I sometimes questioned if I'd made the right choice by staying with my mom after my parents split up. But now that I'm here, I'm starting to think that staying with Mom was the best decision I could have made.

Chapter 10

The café is echoing with laughter when I come in. Carrie's brother Kai is trying to juggle a few balled-up napkins at a time, making Taylor giggle so much that I'm afraid she'll pass out. Carrie and I exchange knowing looks as I fire up the ovens. It's obvious that Kai and Taylor like each other.

After Kai heads off to the smoothie stand, Taylor comes over with a big smile on her face. "Ava," she says. "I got something for you." She pulls a small paper bag out of her pocket.

"For me?"

"I saw it in the gift shop and thought of you."

I can't believe Taylor got me a present when money is so tight at her house. I open the bag and fish around until I pull out a thin chain with a—*ahh!* A ceramic horse's head dangling from it!

I almost shriek and drop it on the floor. What the Shrek is this?

"Can you believe that necklace was on the sale rack?" Taylor says. "It was only a dollar!"

I cough. Even if I really did like horses, I'd find the necklace terrifying. It looks like a decapitated horse's head with wild, terrified eyes.

"Thank you!" I manage to say. She gives me an expectant look, and I realize she's waiting for me to put it on. Reluctantly, I fasten it around my neck. It feels like a big lump of ugly weighing down my chest.

"It's perfect," Taylor announces.

Luckily, before I'm forced to agree with her, Carrie comes over to announce that it's time to get to work. I see her eyes dart to my necklace, and her mouth makes a little "o" of surprise. I rush back to the wall of ovens, wondering when I can take the necklace off without looking rude.

After the ovens are loaded with pastries, Carrie leans on the counter and says, "How are you doing with the Gossip File?"

I shrug. "Not sure yet."

"Let's see what you have," she says, but I shake my head and tell her that it's not ready. "All right," she says, "but this stuff better be good!"

I give her a weak smile and tell her it will be.

"So, Ava," Carrie says after a long pause. "Where are you from?"

"From Massachusetts," I say, taking a tray of cinnamon rolls out of the oven. I shudder to think what they'll taste like—paprika? I've already told Carrie where I live, but even after only knowing her for a day, I'm starting to realize that she isn't always the best listener.

"I mean, where are you from originally?" she says.

"I was born there."

"No," Taylor breaks in. "She means, what nationality are you?"

"Oh." Does Carrie assume that because I look different than she does, that means I wasn't born in the same country? My stomach starts to clench. This is like that stupid guy at the airport all over again. "My mom's parents were both Swedish, and my grandparents on my dad's side are from Korea."

"Have you ever been to Korea?" says Carrie, sounding genuinely interested. My stomach unclenches a little as I realize that she's not trying to make me feel like a freak.

"No, but my dad talks about us going sometime. He's never been either. He was born in California."

"Do you guys eat Korean food at home and stuff?" says Taylor.

I swallow and grab some icing from the fridge. "Sometimes," I say, but it's not really true. A couple of years ago a Korean restaurant opened up in town and we kept talking about going, but then it closed and we never got a chance.

"I wish my family did things like that," says Carrie. "The most exotic my mom gets is when she makes meat loaf and puts pineapple on top. It's disgusting."

"Maybe you can make Korean food for us sometime," says Taylor, her eyes wide with excitement.

"Yeah, maybe," I say weakly.

As I focus on squirting the icing on the cinnamon rolls, it hits me that I've never really thought about the fact that my grandparents came from a different country. I mean, I know they did, and when I see them or talk to them (which isn't very often) they have accents and sometimes speak to each other in Korean. But they're also pretty American. They go out for pizza every Saturday night and send me Santa cards with money in them on Christmas. Last year my grandmother gave me some really strong perfume for my birthday, but I don't know if that's a Korean thing or an old lady thing.

But not knowing how to answer Carrie's and Taylor's

questions makes me feel like I've let my grandparents down somehow, like I should know more about being part Korean than I do.

Just then, a group of people comes in and the breakfast rush officially starts. We work steadily for the next couple of hours. By the end of it, I'm so sick of looking at those trays of foul pastries that I want to scream. It feels like it's been years since I *really* baked something.

"Okay," Carrie announces once the café is empty again. "It's game time. Ava, it's your turn to pick one."

I rack my brain for a minute. Then I realize that games don't always have to involve throwing things. "How about I make some cupcakes and we decorate them."

"How is that a game?" asks Taylor.

"It'll be a contest. We can ask people which ones they like the best."

"So you want us to make cupcakes?" says Carrie, looking skeptical.

"Is that breaking the rules?" I hadn't even thought about that. All I know is that my itch to bake something good is driving me crazy.

She shrugs. "Whatever. I doubt anyone will care. Besides, how else are we going to kill the next couple hours?"

I get to work, poking through the ingredients in the back until I find what I need to make some chocolate and vanilla cupcakes. I add a few spices to the batter to make them a little more interesting. When those are in the oven, I add more butter to the frosting that we use for the donuts to make it creamier. It feels great to be making something I'm excited about for once.

"It smells so good in here," says Taylor when the cupcakes are done baking. "I wish it was like this all the time. Then I might actually want to eat some of the food."

Carrie looks up from noshing on a cookie. "It's not so bad." She laughs at what must be a frown on my face. "My mom thinks sugar is the devil, so she won't let us keep anything like this in the house. That's why I don't mind the stuff here, even if it doesn't actually taste like dessert most of the time."

The timer goes off, meaning the cupcakes are cool enough to decorate. "Okay," I say, grinning with excitement. "We each get five minutes and a plate of cupcakes to decorate. Then we can bring them somewhere—maybe to the salon?—and have people judge them. Ready. Set. Frost!"

All three of us start frantically glopping icing onto the

cupcakes. I try to make mine look like faces because I figure those are the easiest. I make one that looks like Marisol, one that looks like my mom, and one that looks like my dad.

"Are you making troll cupcakes?" Carrie asks, looking over my shoulder.

So much for my artistic talent.

A second later, the timer goes off. "Time's up!" I yell. "Step away from the cupcakes." I'm reminded of the baking competition I did a few weeks ago back home. Luckily this time there's no pressure. In fact, I don't care if I win at all. It's just fun to be goofing off with my new friends.

As we admire our work, the café door swings open. I turn to see Ellie walk in. Oh no. Before I can do anything, Carrie and Taylor grab the plates of cupcakes and shove them under the counter.

"Hi, girls!" Ellie chirps. "I wanted to see how you're all getting along."

"Fine," says Carrie with a tight smile. "Everything's great."

Ellie glances around. "It looks a little empty in here, but it smells fantastic!"

I can feel Carrie and Taylor stiffen beside me, probably getting ready to lie if Ellie asks what's been baking.

"Actually, we were talking about how to fill this place

up," I find myself saying. "We thought about going around the resort this afternoon and giving out pastry samples. That might bring in some business." This must be Ava talking because I'm usually terrible at thinking on my feet.

Ellie's face lights up. "That's a great idea. Nice thinking, Rachel." She gives us a bright smile and walks back out the door.

My stomach drops all the way into my toes. Oh holy buttered linguini. Did she just call me Rachel?

I can't even look at Carrie and Taylor. Now that they know I've been lying to them, they're going to hate me like they hated Melody.

"Oh my gosh," says Taylor after a long minute. "Did you hear that?"

Carrie laughs. "I know! Ava, she doesn't even know your name. Do you see what we're talking about? Ellie's the worst!"

By the looks on their faces, I can tell they're serious. I'm relieved to be off the hook, but I also feel terrible that I got away with the lie.

"Is she really that bad?" I ask.

Taylor shrugs. "She's always kissing up to Mark."

"And you should see what it says about her in the Gossip

File," Carrie says. My ears perk up, but before I can ask what she means, she adds, "That was a good idea about the free samples, Ava. Of course, now we actually have to go around and give them out." She groans.

"Maybe we'll see Kai," Taylor chimes in.

"Okay, ladies," Carrie says, reaching under the counter, "let's see which one of us is the ultimate cupcake champion."

Chapter 11

Halfway through the lunch rush, I realize that Carrie put our cupcakes in the display case. Even though they're hideous, Carrie convinces people to buy them. And one man, after trying the first one, buys two more. Even if we're technically breaking the rules, I have to admit that seeing people enjoying my work makes me feel good. At least that's one thing I have that Ava doesn't. Or maybe we both do. How do people who lead double lives do this? It's so confusing.

When the lunch rush dies down, Carrie holds up some coffee filters and says, "Who wants to play a game? Maybe Floppy Frisbee?"

"Shouldn't we go give away samples?" I ask.

Carrie's face falls. "Oh right. Okay, you two go and I'll keep an eye on the café."

I nod and get to work cutting up some of the pastries I

baked this morning. Then we put them on plates and head out the door.

"While you're out there, see if you can find anything good for the Gossip File," Carrie says. "We're expecting your five bits of juiciness by the end of the week!"

I hurry outside. Maybe if I'm lucky, Ellie will have found someone to take over for me before then and the girls will forget all about it.

"Where to first?" says Taylor, following after me.

"How about the gym?"

"You really think people going to the gym will want pastries?" says Taylor.

I laugh. "Why do you think they're working out in the first place?"

She smiles, and we head in that direction. After we get set up, Taylor starts chatting with anyone who walks by, even the landscaping crew. I try to smile and hand out pastries. Talking to strangers is so not my forte. But then again, I'm not me. I'm Ava. Maybe she's better at this kind of thing than I am.

"Excuse me," I say to a friendly looking man who's hurrying toward the bistro. "Would you like to try a cinnamon chip scone?"

"Sorry," he says with an apologetic smile. "I'm not a big fan of the café food." Then he rushes past and heads into the bistro.

So much for trying to improve our reputation.

I scan the area and am surprised to see my dad heading in my direction. "Dad!" I call, waving.

When he spots me, his face lights up. "Hey, Roo," he says. "What are you doing out here?"

As he comes up to me, I realize that he's wearing a red shirt that perfectly matches the one Ellie was wearing this morning. That has to be a coincidence, right? They can't be one of those disgusting matchy-matchy couples.

"I'm giving away samples," I tell him. "Want to try one?"

He smiles and pops one in his mouth. As he swallows, though, his smile fades. "Hmm, this kind of tastes like... parsley. Not one of your creations, is it?"

I shake my head. "The café won't let us make anything from scratch."

"That's too bad. I'm sure they have a reason for it."

"So what are you doing here?"

"Bringing Ellie some lunch." He holds up a takeout bag. "Like I do every Tuesday."

Date night on Monday, lunch on Tuesday, and pizza

night every week? "I thought you were really busy with work," I say.

"I am," he responds, "but I try to sneak away once in a while to make time for Ellie."

Something stabs at me. My dad can make time for Ellie every week, but I've come all this way and he can't even make time for me?

"Maybe we could go out for ice cream tonight after dinner," I say. "Just the two of us?" Ice cream has always been our thing. He can't say no to that, can he?

Dad nods absently and checks his watch. "We'll talk about it later, okay?"

"Or mini-golf!" I say. "We haven't done that in years. Maybe we can go later? Or tomorrow?"

"Sure, Roo. But I have to go." He gives me a quick kiss on the forehead and hurries off. As he walks away, I can't help feeling that I'm looking at a stranger. He might look like my dad and sound like my dad, but whoever this person is, I'm meeting him for the first time.

● ● ●

After Taylor and I get back to the café, I have to wait an hour before I can go through the Gossip File while Carrie and Taylor aren't looking. My heart is pounding as I flip through it, searching for Ellie's name and whatever bad thing Carrie said is written about her.

It takes me a while to find it, but finally I spot a page of scratchy writing with "Ellie" underlined about halfway down. I glance around to make sure Carrie and Taylor are still in the back of the café, and then I start reading.

"Ellie gets her hair done at the salon every morning, but she still looks like a mess. She pretends she's perfect, but she's not. Pretty soon, people are going to catch on to what she's really like."

Wow, whoever wrote this stuff about Ellie really didn't like her.

I flip the page, hoping for more, but that's all it says. I hear Taylor pirouetting across the café, so I quickly shut the book and shove it back into its hiding spot. Then I pretend to wipe down the counter, realizing too late that I'm holding a plastic bag instead of a rag.

"Um, are you okay?" Taylor asks.

"I'm fine," I say, but it doesn't sound all that convincing. I can't ignore the icky feeling that's been growing inside me ever since I saw my dad earlier.

"You seem kind of distracted. And you barely even looked at people when we were handing out the pastries earlier."

"I'm just…" Part of me is tempted to tell Taylor what's going on, but I can't explain to her that my dad is seeing Ellie. That would only make everything more complicated.

Luckily, Carrie saves me from having to say anything as she rushes over, untying her apron. "It's four o'clock. Time to go, ladies. If you want to clean up, I'll do the registers."

When we're done closing up, we troop outside into the crazy humidity, and Carrie locks the café door. She turns to me. "Do you want to hang out with us tonight? I think we're going to see a movie and get out of the heat for a while."

"Oh, I can't. I have plans."

"Maybe tomorrow," says Carrie brightly. "It would be fun to hang out." She puts one arm around my shoulder and the other around Taylor's. "I could use some cheering up."

"Why? What's going on?" says Taylor.

Carrie sighs. "My mom's been giving me a hard time about college again." She looks at me and explains, "She really wants me to go, but we can't afford it. No matter how many hours I work, it's not going to be enough, you know? But she can't accept that. She wants me to get a second job."

"Wow," says Taylor. "What does your dad say?"

Carrie snorts. "What does my dad ever say? 'I don't

know. Go ask your mother. Where did I put my socks?' The man hasn't had a clue since before I was born."

I think about the way my parents were before they split up. They never argued, not really, but they never actually talked, either. It sounds like Carrie's parents aren't that different from mine.

"You'll figure it out," I tell her. "Maybe you need to take a year off after high school and earn money for college. That's what my mom did." I don't mention that my mom wound up meeting my dad, getting married, and having me instead.

Carrie gives me a bright smile. "That's what I've been thinking. Thanks, Ava."

Even though it's been a rough day, I can't help smiling. At least I have some new friends to help make things a little better. At this point, Ava's life is going a whole lot better than mine.

Chapter 12

My mom calls as I'm getting ready for dinner. I keep fidgeting with my new yellow dress, adjusting the neckline since it's lower than what I'd normally wear. At least I could finally take off the hideous necklace Taylor gave me.

I don't really feel like talking to Mom—what if she asks about Ellie?—but if I ignore her call, she'll keep trying until she reaches me.

"Rachel! It's so great to hear your voice!" Mom says when I pick up, even though I called her yesterday. "How are things going?"

"Good. I'm still having fun."

"That's it? Tell me everything. Are you using lots of sunscreen?" she says.

"Yeah, Mom." Part of me wants to tell her about how weird Dad's been acting around Ellie, but I don't want her to get mad at him. Besides, the last thing I want to do is talk to my mom about my dad's new girlfriend—awkward! Instead, I blurt out, "I've been working a lot, so I haven't been in the sun all that—"

"Working? Working on what?"

I clear my throat. I've been afraid to tell my mom about the job in case it's yet another reason for her to be upset with my dad. "I volunteered to do it," I tell her. "They were really short-staffed at the resort café, so I'm helping out for a couple of days."

"But you're supposed to be on vacation! What about all the things you wanted to do with your father?"

"I know, but we'll have plenty of time for that later." Ick. I sound just like him.

Mom sighs. "I don't like this. You tell your dad that if he makes you work the whole time—"

"He won't! Besides, it's not so bad. At least I have some extra spending money."

"Do you need more money?" Mom says. "Is your father not giving you enough? I can send you some."

Oh boy. I should have known better than to mention the M-word. "No, it's fine. Really. Mom, you don't have to worry!"

She laughs, but I can hear tears in her voice. "How can I not worry? My baby is a thousand miles away!"

"How's apartment hunting?" I ask, trying to change the subject before she starts sobbing into my ear. Then I might start crying too.

She sighs. "I haven't had time to look at a single place. The cleaning business has me pretty busy. If this keeps up, we might not need to sell the house after all."

My heart leaps. I'd told Mom I was okay with us putting our house on the market since renting a smaller place would mean her not having to worry about money all the time, but we've lived in that house since I was three. Of course I want us to stay if we can.

"So the business is really doing okay?" I ask. After how much we struggled to keep clients this summer, it's great to hear my mom sounding optimistic again.

"So far so good! It still feels strange not to go to the law office every morning, but I'm getting used to it. And I'm learning so much from Ladybug Cleaners about running a business. We'll definitely be busy when you get home. Which is one reason I wanted you to get a real vacation before school starts!"

"Mom..." I don't want to have the same discussion all

over again. Just then, there's a knock on my door and Ellie pokes her head in. "Mom, I have to go. We're about to have dinner."

"Okay, I'm glad we got to talk. Call me tomorrow if you have time, okay? Or even tonight. I'll be here! Oh, honey, I miss you so much. Try to have some fun, okay?"

"I will, Mom. I miss you too."

When I hang up the phone, I notice Ellie giving me a wistful look from the doorway. "You really love her, don't you?" she says.

"What?" Suddenly, I realize that she's wearing the purple version of the dress that she gave me. Creepy.

"Your mom," Ellie says. "I can tell you really care about her." For once she isn't smiling or laughing. She has a faraway look on her face. "I wish Caleb felt that way about me."

I study my shoes, feeling awkward. I could try to assure her that Caleb does love her, but the only thing he seems to care about is his iPad.

"Anyhoo," Ellie says after a second, snapping back to reality. "Your dad should be here at seven with the pizza. Want to help Caleb set the table?"

I almost shriek when I see that Caleb is wearing a

striped shirt that matches Ellie's and my outfits. Together, we look like the cast of a musical or something.

I grab a pile of plates and start putting them out on the table, while Caleb slowly walks around laying out silver-ware with one hand and tapping away on his tablet with the other.

"What are you always playing on there?" I finally ask.

"I'm not playing," he says. "I'm designing."

"Designing what?"

He sighs like I've asked the stupidest question on earth. Then he shows me the screen, revealing a 3-D model of some kind of medieval torture device. "It's a trebuchet," he says.

"A what?"

"It's a type of catapult, but it uses a counterweight instead of a spring. I'm designing and building a miniature one for the festival. I bet no one will make one of these, so I'll win the contest for sure."

"Why do you care so much about winning?" I ask. "It doesn't seem like the festival is going to be all that big." In fact, from what I've seen, it might be a total mess.

He shrugs and doesn't say anything for so long that I start to think he won't answer at all. Then he glances over his shoulder, as if making sure Ellie isn't listening, and says softly, "Because if I win, maybe my dad will notice."

"Notice that you won? Of course he'll notice."

"No," Caleb says, his voice still soft. "He's always working on these awesome projects all over the world. Whenever I show him sketches of stuff I've designed, he says they're good, but I can tell he doesn't mean it. If I won the contest, maybe I'd finally prove to him that I can be as good as he is."

Since things with my dad are so weird right now, I can actually relate to what Caleb is saying. For years, Mom and I struggled to find some common ground, but now I feel like we're on the same island while Dad is out in the ocean, floating away on a raft.

"You'll find a way to get through to your dad," I say. Hopefully, we both will.

At exactly 7 p.m., there's a knock on the door and Dad comes in holding a couple of pizza boxes. He clearly just got back from his scuba trip. He's still a little sandy-looking, and his black hair is wet with sweat.

"Sorry," he says when he gives me a damp hug. "I didn't have time to shower. But I come bearing dinner!"

He looks exhausted, but I'm glad to see him, sweaty and

all. "It's no worse than when we spent all day raking leaves and then went to Molly's Diner for ice cream, remember?" I say.

Dad laughs, the first genuine laugh I've heard in days. "I miss Molly's. There are lots of ice-cream places here, but none of them taste the same as that. Plus"—he winks— "no one here can keep up with my ice-cream appetite like you can."

"Are you saying I'm an ice-cream piggy?" I say, making an oinking sound.

Dad laughs and oinks back at me. For a second it feels like I have my old dad back. Then Ellie sends him off to get changed for dinner, and he comes back wearing a striped shirt just like Caleb's. I stare at it in horror as Ellie giggles and announces she has to take a picture of all of us.

"We look like an adorable little family!" she says as she makes us cluster together. Is this what she thinks a family is? People who hang out all the time and wear matching outfits? I'm pretty sure that's called a cult.

When we sit down for dinner, I wind up all the way on the other end of the table from Dad. I watch in disgust as he and Ellie whisper things to each other and laugh. I bet she can't eat even half of the ice cream that my dad and I can.

When we're almost done with dinner, Ellie seems to finally notice that there are other people at the table. "Rachel," she says, "how did the pastry samples work out today?"

"Good. People took them." I don't add that they didn't seem all that impressed once they tried them. "But I was thinking, what if the café made food from scratch? All the other Four Palms restaurants do it."

Ellie shakes her head. "It's more cost effective as is. Trust me, Mark has it all figured out."

"Carrie said the café has been struggling to stay open. Don't you think more people will come in if the food is really good?" I ask.

"But it *is* good. Isn't it?" she asks, making it sound like I hurt her feelings.

"Yeah," I say through my teeth. "I was thinking…if you wanted to try something new…"

"I appreciate it, Rachel," Ellie says. "I'll certainly mention it to Mark, but the resort has done things a certain way for years. I doubt they'd be up for trying anything new, especially not when we're so short-handed. Once you go home, I'll have to scramble to fill your position as it is."

"But you're doing that now, right?" I say. "I can't stay there the whole two weeks."

"Of course not!" says Ellie. "And I wouldn't expect you to. We'll figure things out soon. I promise."

I'm starting to wonder if Ellie's promises are just as empty as my dad's. I glance over at Caleb who's busily stacking his pizza crusts into an arch. Maybe I should be more like him: ignore my parents and just focus on my own stuff. But it's all an act, I have to remind myself. He wants his dad's attention as much as I want mine's.

"Dad," I say, "have you figured out when we can go to Disney? We need to go soon if we want to see everything." I start listing the rides and attractions we have to check out while we're there. "And after that, we have to do SeaWorld and—"

"Whoa," he says. "That sounds like a lot. Keep in mind we'll only have one day."

I feel like someone punched me in the gut. "Only one day? What do you mean?"

Dad sighs and looks at Ellie as if he's searching for help, like he can't even remember how to talk to me anymore.

"Rachel, don't forget that your father has to work," she says, but I ignore her. This is none of her business.

"Dad, you said you could get a few days off," I say. "You promised we'd do the trip like we always planned. I had a whole bunch of stuff we were going to do, and so far we haven't done a single one. We've been talking about this trip since I was six years old!"

Everyone at the table looks at me, even Caleb. I realize how whiny I sound, but how can Dad just throw away my dream like that? How are we ever supposed to be able to talk to each other again when we can't even spend any real time together?

"I'm sorry," he says finally. "I'm doing the best I can." He sounds like he means it, like he really believes it. And maybe he is doing the best he can, but it doesn't feel like nearly enough.

Chapter 13

After we're done cleaning up from dinner, Dad turns to me and says, "Roo, you said something about going mini-golfing tonight."

My heart swells with hope. Finally, Dad and I are going to have some one-on-one time!

Then Ellie chimes in with "I think it's a great idea! Let's go now!" and ruins everything.

My mouth sags open. "But, Dad—"

"It'll be fun if we all go," he says softly. "We'll do something with just you and me another time, okay?"

I don't get it. Does Dad not want to spend time with me? Am I doing something wrong? The worst part is that I can't even ask him these questions because what if he's realized he doesn't like having me here? What if I'm interfering with his new life? If that's how he feels, all I can do is try to show him that having me come visit was worth it. So

I smile and climb into the car with grumpy ol' Caleb, and we head to a mini-golf place a few miles away.

When we get there, Ellie insists on getting a green ball even though I try to explain to her that it's always Dad's color.

"No problem," he says. "I think I'll go with red today. Change is good for the soul."

As we head to the first hole, Ellie grabs the scorecard and declares that she's going to keep score so that none of us can cheat. I don't know why anyone would care enough to cheat in mini-golf, but she seems determined that we do everything the "right way."

But as we start to play, I have a sneaking suspicion that Ellie's never even been on a mini-golf course before. Every time she goes to hit the ball, she misses or hits it in the grass. And one time, she even manages to smack it backward so that it sails all the way to the beginning of the course and then disappears in the water. Poor Dad has to spend ten minutes fishing it out, even though I try to tell Ellie that she should just go ask for another ball.

"That's all right," she says. "My knight will take care of it."

Gross.

"Isn't this fun?" she asks as we finally move on to the next hole. "The perfect family outing!"

If she calls us a family one more time, I might actually scream. Meanwhile, Caleb measures each shot from every angle to see which one will get the best results. We take so long at each hole that we have to let three other groups of people skip ahead of us.

I can't help imagining what this would have been like with just Dad and me. We wouldn't care about keeping score or about getting every shot. We'd just be laughing and chatting and acting goofy. Will we ever have a chance to do that again?

Finally, we get to the last hole and the torture ends. Caleb ends up winning, Dad and I tie for second, and Ellie winds up with such a high score that there isn't enough room to write it on the card.

"Should we head over to my place for some dessert?" Dad asks.

"Teddy, we don't have to go squish into that tiny apartment," Ellie says, wrinkling her nose. "We could go out for dessert or back to my place or—"

"I want to see where my dad lives!" I say. I don't care if

his apartment is smaller than an airplane bathroom. I can't go back home without ever setting eyes on it.

We pile into Ellie's car and head toward Dad's place. One of the dozens of things I've missed about my dad since he's been gone has been his stories. I ask him to tell us about some of the wacky tourists he's mentioned to me on the phone, but Ellie jumps in instead.

"Just last week your father had a man asking if he'd see any kangaroos during the snorkeling trip," she says.

"Kangaroos?" Caleb says. "Don't they only have those in Australia?"

"And since when do kangaroos live in the water?" I add, looking at my dad.

"Exactly!" he starts to say, but Ellie cuts him off.

"It turns out the man had heard about tree kangaroos and figured they must be able to live anywhere, even in the ocean," she says. "I guess he didn't realize he was on the wrong continent."

Ellie giggles loudly while my dad lets out a soft chuckle. I force myself to smile, but really I want to yell, "Dad, why can't you tell your own stories? Why are you letting Ellie take over everything?"

When we get to his apartment, I'm expecting someplace

tiny, but I'm still shocked when we go into what's essentially a long hallway with a sofa shoved into it. Off the bigger hallway are a smaller hallway with Dad's bed and an even smaller one with a kitchen jammed inside. As we get the "grand tour," I find myself shuffling sideways the whole time like a crab. No wonder my dad decided to let me stay with Ellie! Otherwise, I would've had to sleep standing up in the kitchen.

"Wow," I say slowly. "This is…nice."

Dad shrugs. "It was the best I could do at first. Now that work has been steadier at the resort, I should be able to upgrade soon."

Ellie giggles. "But this place has so much charm!" She jokingly caresses the hideous green wallpaper while Caleb rolls his eyes and goes to turn on the TV.

"Who wants ice cream?" Dad asks.

Since his apartment only has one measly window AC unit sputtering away against the heat, we all instantly raise our hands.

Caleb and Ellie go to sit on the tiny balcony to cool down while I squeeze into the kitchen and help my dad scoop some chocolate chip ice cream. After a minute, I take a deep breath and say, "Dad? I, um, wanted to talk to you about something."

He sighs and puts down his spoon. "I know I've been working too much, and I'm sorry. The thing is, if I want to get to where I'd like to be in life, that means making sacrifices, even if that includes—"

"No, Dad," I say, not sure what he's talking about. "It's about Ellie."

He holds up his hands like he's surrendering. "I can guess what you're going to say, and I understand that you don't want to spend your vacation working, but she really needs your help and—"

"Dad! Listen!" I say in a loud whisper. Ellie's still outside, but I definitely don't want her to hear me. "It's not about work. It's about… Do you think you'll marry Ellie?"

Dad lets out a surprised cough. "Where is this coming from?"

"I just wondered, that's all. Have you guys talked about it?"

Weirdly, his cheeks get a little red. I can probably count on my fingers the number of times I've seen my dad blush. My cheeks get hot too. Apparently, I'm a sympathy blusher.

"There's nothing in the plans now," he says slowly, "but I think one day, it's a definite possibility."

That sounds like a long way of saying "yes."

"You'd be okay with that, wouldn't you, Roo?" Dad adds.

It's my turn to let out a surprised cough. "Oh, um. I mean, Ellie seems nice and everything, but don't you think she's sort of taken over?"

He blinks at me. "Taken over?"

"Yeah. I mean, look at how she was telling your stories for you on the way here."

Dad smiles. "Roo, that's just how she is. She loves telling stories."

"No, it's more than that. She has this list of stuff the two of you have to do, but what about me? I mean, I'm only here for a couple weeks, and you're spending more time with her than you are with me."

"I was afraid this might happen." He lets out a long, tired-sounding sigh. "It's normal for you to be jealous. You two just need to get used to each other, that's all."

"Dad, that's not it! You should hear what the girls at work say about her, and there's this notebook at the café that says she's not as perfect as she seems, and—"

"Enough, Rachel," he says. "Ellie is a sweet woman. I don't want you saying anything else about her." He puts down the ice-cream scoop. "Maybe this trip was a mistake. You weren't ready to see me with someone else yet."

"What? No, that's not it."

"Roo, it's okay. I understand. In your place, I'd probably feel the same way. But let's try to make the best of it, okay? Can you do that for me?"

I can't believe it. Has my dad heard a single word I've said? I don't know where my old dad went, the one I could talk to about anything, but he's clearly not here with me right now.

"Fine," I finally say, because he's waiting for an answer. "I'll make the best of it."

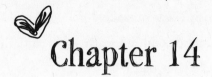

Chapter 14

That night, I can't fall asleep. Not only do I keep think-ing I can hear the ground groaning under my bed—a sinkhole brewing under the building, waiting to slurp me up—but I can't help wondering if coming to Florida *was* a huge mistake. Maybe Dad is right. He doesn't have time for me, and my dream of going to Disney feels like it's never going to come true. We're practically down the road from Epcot, and I might never actually see it. Even if we do go, how can I enjoy myself and find a way to reconnect with my dad when Ellie keeps getting in the way?

Finally, even though it's late, I call Marisol, hoping she's still up and that her phone ringing won't wake up her parents.

"Rachel? Are you okay?" she whispers when she answers it.

"I…I don't know," I whisper back. "I tried to talk to my

dad about stuff tonight, but he got all defensive and said me coming to visit was a mistake."

I hear Marisol suck in a breath. "He said that? That doesn't sound like your dad."

"None of this sounds like my dad! I don't know what happened to him. I'm not even sure he wants me here."

Marisol chuckles. "Are you kidding? He's been saying for months how much he wants you to come visit."

"That's the thing. He's been saying it, but he hasn't been acting like it. He's barely spent any time with me, and when he and I are together, it's like we don't know how to talk to each other. He's not the same person he was a few months ago."

"Or maybe *you're* not," she says.

"What do you mean?"

"Think about everything that's happened since your dad left. There's no way you're the same person that you were then. And maybe he's been through stuff that's changed him too. You guys just have to get to know each other again."

"If he marries Ellie, that might never happen. You should have heard him today, Marisol. If Ellie proposes, I know he'll say yes."

"I'm sorry," she says, and I'm shocked to realize that even she's stumped by the whole situation. The fact that Marisol, who always has an encouraging word or bit of advice, sounds defeated makes me feel even worse.

"I wish you could have come down here with me," I say. "This vacation would have been a ton better with you around."

"But then you'd be working all the time and I'd be lounging by the pool all day. I'd be so bored."

"Oh yeah," I say with a snort. "That sounds horrible. Poor you."

She laughs. "Anyway, if talking to your dad didn't work, maybe you should try talking to Ellie."

"That won't be awkward. 'Hey, Ellie. Can you get your claws out of my dad so I can hang out with him?'"

"It's either that or things stay the same," she says.

Ugh. She's right. I guess I'll have to swallow my mortification and give it a try.

● ● ●

When I get to Ellie's office in the morning, I'm about to knock on the half-open door. Then I hear her voice inside, sounding surprisingly angry, and I freeze.

"But what about Caleb?" she says. "What am I supposed

to tell him?" She's quiet for a minute like she's on the phone, and then she says, "He doesn't want to be here. He wants to be with you. And now I'm supposed to tell him that his father would rather take on a new project than spend time with him?"

Another long pause and finally she sighs and says, "All right. I'll think of something to tell him. But I hope you realize what you're doing. That boy idolizes you, and you're just throwing him away the way you threw away our relationship." Then she slams down the phone.

I stand there like a statue for a minute, digesting what I heard. Caleb seems convinced that his father is an amazing guy, but maybe Ellie is the one who's really on his side.

As I'm trying to decide if I should run away or knock and do what I came here to do, I hear Ellie get out of her chair and cross the room. If she takes one more step toward me, she'll see me standing here. So I quickly pound on the door, like I can't wait to talk to her.

"Oh, Rachel!" she says in surprise as she appears in the doorway. "Come in. Sit down." She shows me into her office, which is tiny and littered with empty iced-coffee cups. Not exactly the neat and perfect workspace I was expecting.

"What an interesting necklace!" Ellie says when I'm slumped into the chair opposite hers. The anger in her voice is gone, like it was never there.

"Um, thanks." I finger the horrible horse necklace that's somehow even heavier and more terrifying than it was yesterday. I really didn't want to put it on this morning, but I was afraid Taylor would be offended if I didn't.

"So what can I do for you?" she asks.

Just be Ava, I tell myself. No, I haven't developed multiple personalities, but Ava is a whole lot better at talking to people than I am. I could use her boost of confidence right now.

"I wanted to talk to you," I squeak. I go to spout the words I rehearsed in the shower this morning, but instead I find myself saying, "It's about me working so much." Wait. Where did that come from?

"Ah." She leans back in her chair. "I was afraid this might happen. You know, when I first started working here, I had a hard time fitting in too. But eventually, I made some friends and it all started to come together. Just be yourself and people will realize how lovely you really are."

I stare at her. "Actually," I say, "the people here like me just fine. In fact, I think this is the most popular I've ever been." I realize as I say it how snotty that sounds, but come on. Why did Ellie have to assume that the other girls think I'm a loser?

"Oh," she says. "So what's the problem?"

"I wanted to make sure you're looking for someone to take my job. You said I'd be at the café for a couple of days, and it's been three."

"Well, to be honest with you, Rachel, it's been hard to find someone. But I'm looking, I promise. And if we can't find someone by next week, the café will just manage without you, okay?"

I let out a long sigh of relief. "Thank you." If I have to spend my whole vacation working, not only will I never have time to reconnect with Dad, but I'll feel even more cheated.

Ellie looks at her watch. "Do you mind if I send you off to the café? The morning rush should be starting soon."

"No, wait!"

Her eyebrows shoot up. "What's the matter?"

Just say it, I tell myself. *Just casually bring it up and see what she says.* "I need to ask you something else...about my dad."

Her face relaxes. "Of course. I could talk about your

father all day." Since I've heard how much she talks, I don't doubt it.

I clear my throat. "Well, I've been trying to convince him that we should go to Disney for a few days, but he never has any time."

"He's been so busy at work—"

"It's not just that! It's…it's you!" I blurt out. "With your date nights and your pizza and stuff. How am I supposed to hang out with him when you're taking up all his time?" So much for being casual.

Ellie gives me a long look. "I'm sorry you feel that way, Rachel. Of course I don't want to come between you and your father, but we're going to be family soon. Don't you think we should get used to sharing him?"

But I don't want to share him! my brain screams. Not all the time, anyway. "I've been planning this trip to Disney with him since I was little," I say. "I've come all this way. It *has* to happen."

I can hear how desperate my voice sounds, and I guess it must get through to Ellie because she finally says, "You're right. If you want to go to Disney, then we'll go to Disney."

Oh my goldfish. Why does she have to always assume

that she's invited to everything? Can't I have even one day alone with my dad?

"Wait!" Ellie adds, sitting up in her seat. "It would be the perfect spot! Why didn't I think of it before? I mean, Disney *is* supposed to be the most magical place on earth."

"Perfect spot for what?" I say.

"For me to propose to your father!" she says.

All I can do is stare at her, my breath frozen in my chest like it's been glued there.

"Don't say a word to him, okay? I want it to be a complete surprise." She checks her watch again. "Oops! It's getting late. We don't want to leave Carrie and Taylor all alone during the rush, do we?" She shoos me toward the door. "Don't worry, Rachel. Just leave all the planning to me," Ellie adds, giving me a little wink before she shuts the door in my face.

Chapter 15

While Taylor is eating lunch and Carrie is checking stock in the back, I sneak under the counter and grab the Gossip File. At this point, I'm desperate. There has to be something in here that can help me break up my dad and Ellie.

As the thought forms in my head, I realize that as bad as it sounds, that's exactly what I have to do. I can't let Ellie ruin everything. My dad can't be happy with her when he never jokes around and works all the time and does what she wants every second of the day. Once Ellie is out of his life, I'll be able to get my old dad back.

I flip through the notes, trying to make sense of things like: "Girl in purple with blue icing," and slogging my way through boring stuff like "Kai got to the smoothie stand at 8:05 a.m., two minutes later than yesterday." I think Harriet the Spy would be a little disappointed.

I try to find more things about Ellie, but there's nothing useful except for what I saw last time about her not being what she seems.

I'm just about to slam the book shut in frustration when something catches my eye under a section titled "Amir."

"Ellie dumped Amir today. She waited until his shift at FP Sushi ended, and then she gave him the ring back in front of everyone. He begged her to change her mind, but she said that his kids were a deal breaker."

The entry is dated last August, almost exactly a year ago.

Oh my goldfish. Does this mean Ellie was engaged to someone else at the resort? "FP Sushi" has to mean Four Palms Sushi. I scan the rest of the Amir notes, but there's nothing else except one mention of his twin sons.

My head is pounding as I shove the Gossip File under the counter. Then I head to the back of the café and peek my head into the storeroom.

"What are we ever going to do with ten pounds of granola?" Carrie says with a laugh, pointing to a giant container in the corner. "I'm pretty sure that stuff's been here as long as I've been alive. Maybe we should have thrown it into the sinkhole."

"Hey, Carrie," I say. "Do you know a guy named Amir?"

She thinks for a second. "You mean Amir who works at the sushi place? I think he's the manager or something."

"Yes!" I say. "He's still there?"

"I think so. I think I've only met him a couple of times." Her brow furrows. "I think he was dating Ellie for a while. But who cares about that, right?"

"No. I want to hear more about it."

"I'm not really the person to ask. If you want the dirt on the whole thing, why not just ask Amir?"

It's my turn to laugh. "Yeah, right. I can't ask a total stranger about his ex-girlfriend."

Carrie shrugs. "I guess that would be awkward."

And yet…what choice do I have? Maybe if I can find out what happened between Ellie and Amir, it'll help me figure out what to do. At this point, I don't know if I can save my vacation, but at least I can still save my dad.

* * *

As I'm leaving the cafe, my phone rings. It's Evan.

"Hey, Booger Crap," he says when I answer. I can actually hear him grinning. "How are things going?"

"Um, okay," I say, which feels like a lie. There's so much to tell him that I don't even know where to start. "I'm not sure about my dad and Ellie, but otherwise things are good."

"What happened?" he says.

"She, um...I think she's going to ask him to marry her...at Disney."

Evan sucks in a breath. "Really? Wow."

"Yeah."

"But that's not so bad, right?" he says. "I mean, your mom found someone new too. And your parents are almost divorced."

"You don't understand. Ellie's... She wants everything to be some bizarro version of perfect. She pretends that family is the most important thing to her, but I just found out she dumped a guy last year because of his kids. You should see how she is, always telling my dad what to do, taking over his whole life. If my dad marries her, I might never see the real him again!"

"So what are you going to do?" Evan knows me well enough by now to guess that I won't sit by and do nothing.

"What I always do," I say, chuckling. "Fumble around doing stupid things until I make a total mess."

Evan doesn't laugh. Instead, he says, "I know you want to help, but be careful."

He's right. I've learned my lesson about sneaky schemes,

but I need to do something to help my dad. Otherwise, I might lose him forever.

"I will," I tell Evan.

But as I hang up, I realize that I can't afford to be careful, not when I only have ten days left to get my dad to see the truth about Ellie.

Instead of heading to my room, I go over to Four Palms Sushi. It's pretty empty since it's still early, so it doesn't take me long to find Amir talking to one of the sushi chefs. I hover in the corner until he's done and then force myself to go over. *Pretend you're Ava*, I tell myself. *She'll know what to say.*

"Amir?" I ask.

"Yes?"

"Hi, I'm um…doing a story for my school paper about romance in the workplace. Could I interview you?" For some reason, I find myself doing a cheesy reporter voice.

His forehead wrinkles. "Why do you want to interview me?"

"Well, I heard you were engaged to someone who works here, but she dumped you because of your kids." *Smooth, Rachel. Way to pour salt on his wounds.*

"Who told you that?"

"Oh, um, someone in the kitchen. Anyway, is it true? What happened between you two?"

Amir blinks at me for a second. "I'd really rather not talk about it," he says. "She's happy now. That's all that matters."

"You want Ellie to be happy? Even after she dumped you?"

"She didn't dump me," he says. "It was a mutual agreement."

"But I heard—"

"People here love to gossip," he says, "but believe me, I cared about Ellie a great deal. I still do. I think she's a wonderful person. We just weren't right for each other, that's all."

"Why, because she tried to change your family so it would be her idea of perfect?" The bitterness in my voice surprises me. I keep telling myself that the worst thing about Ellie is that she's making my dad act like a different person, but it doesn't help that she seems to be trying to change both of us. Clearly, my dad and I aren't good enough the way we are.

Amir's face darkens. "Things *were* easier when my sons weren't with me," he admits. "They live with their mother half the time. When they were visiting, it was harder to make things work. But if Ellie and I had stayed together, I'm sure we would have figured it out eventually."

"But what if you hadn't? Would you still have married her?" I can't believe I'm asking this, but I have to know.

"Wait, which school are you doing this interview for?" he says. "It's summer vacation."

"It's for summer school. I, um, failed my journalism class so I'm taking it over again."

He flashes me a doubtful look and says, "I think those are enough questions for now." Then he gives a little nod and rushes away.

"Dad, wait!" I call after him. I clap my hand over my mouth. Holy fried pickles. I just called a complete stranger "Dad"!

Everyone in the restaurant stares at me as I run for the door. Guaranteed, rumors will be flying across the resort tomorrow about Amir's "mystery daughter." Maybe I should write about *that* in the Gossip File.

Chapter 16

I expect Ellie to make an excuse to have my dad all to herself that night, so I'm not surprised when she calls me from work a couple hours before we're supposed to eat.

"Let me guess," I say. "Something came up and you can't do dinner?"

Ellie laughs like that's the most ridiculous idea she's ever heard. "What? No! I'm just confirming for tonight. How does sushi sound?"

I start to choke. "Sushi?"

"Is that okay? The restaurant at the resort has the best sushi in town."

"No! That's great!" Can this really be a coincidence? Or does Ellie already know about my conversation with Amir? But if she does, why on earth would she want us to go there?

"I have to work late tonight, so let's all just meet at the restaurant at seven thirty. See you in a bit!"

I shake my head as I hang up the phone. What am I supposed to do if Amir talks to me tonight? Do I pretend I don't know him? Then again, maybe Ellie will avoid talking to him all together since he's her ex-fiancé. If I'm lucky, he won't even be there.

A couple hours later, Ellie, Caleb, and I are all standing in the entrance of the restaurant, impatiently tapping our toes. Dad is running late, and Ellie is starting to look really annoyed. Then she glances across the restaurant and her eyes light up.

"Amir!" she calls.

"I thought that was you out here," he says, coming over with a big smile.

I hide my face with my hand and try my best to blend into the wall, hoping Ellie doesn't think to introduce us. Luckily, Amir is too busy grinning at her to even notice me standing a few feet away from him.

"Kids," Ellie says to us, "I'll be right back." Then she pulls Amir a few steps away, and they start chatting like old friends. I guess he was telling the truth about still caring about her.

As I watch them laughing together, I wonder if my dad knows that Ellie was engaged before and broke it off.

Would knowing that fact change his mind about wanting to marry her one day?

I cross my fingers that Dad will come in as Ellie and Amir are talking. Then I could "helpfully" clue him in about their past relationship. But about thirty seconds before Dad finally rushes in, Amir gives Ellie one last smile and heads past the hostess stand. Ugh. Too late.

As we sit down to dinner, Dad apologizes about ten times for being late. Ellie looks annoyed again, even though a minute ago she was laughing with Amir as if she'd forgotten all about Dad not being on time.

"You know how much I hate tardiness," she says.

"I know, honey," Dad says. "At least I let you know I was running late, right?"

Ellie lets out a long sigh. "It's just...after all the times I've been kept waiting in my life..."

I expect her to finish, but she doesn't. Instead, she shakes her head and looks at the menu.

"Dad never did it on purpose," Caleb suddenly chimes in.

Ellie glances up. "What was that?"

"You said you were sick of people keeping you waiting. Obviously, you were talking about Dad. But he never wanted to be late. He just had to work."

"Yes," Ellie says, her voice soft. "Work always comes first for him." Then she shakes her head as if she's clearing it and starts chattering on about what she's going to order.

Caleb sighs and goes back to his 3-D model. If only he knew about the conversation I overheard between his parents, maybe he wouldn't always take his dad's side. But I doubt he'd believe me even if I did tell him the truth.

"Oh, Teddy!" Ellie suddenly announces. "Rachel and I were chatting earlier, and we decided we'd all go to Disney this weekend." She gives me a big wink across the table.

"All of us?" Dad says.

"Can we really go?" Caleb says, perking up. Apparently, he's as excited about amusement parks as he is about catapults.

"It's pretty pricey." Dad scratches his head. "And with all the long lunches I've been taking recently, I'm not sure I can afford the time off..."

"Come on, Teddy," says Ellie. "This is Rachel's vacation. We can splurge a little."

"Let's talk about this later," Dad says, clearly uncomfortable to be talking about money and family stuff in public.

"What's there to talk about? Rachel is here for the perfect family vacation, and that's exactly what we should give her!"

I expect Dad to say something, but he stays quiet, like he's shut down. I don't get it. If my parents were having this conversation, it would have already turned into an argument. They only have to *smell* money and they launch into a heated discussion.

Meanwhile, I don't know what I'm hoping will happen. Of course I want us to go to Disney, but not so that Ellie can do some big marriage proposal on top of Epcot. Figures that she'd take my perfect Disney trip and make it about her.

Just then, I see Amir making his way across the restaurant.

"Ellie," I say, "isn't that the guy you were talking to earlier? Who is he, anyway?"

Her smile fades a little bit. "Oh, just an old friend," she says.

"Is he an ex-boyfriend or something?" I ask.

That gets Dad's attention. He glances in the same direction that I'm looking. "That's right," he says. "I forgot your ex works here. Is that Amir?"

"I bumped into him before dinner," Ellie says. "He seems to be doing well. If he comes by again, I'll introduce you."

"Dad, you—you know about Amir?" I ask.

Dad shrugs. "Of course I do, Roo. Ellie and I don't have any secrets from each other. Do we, sweetheart?" He reaches over and takes her hand, his dark mood suddenly gone. "And I think Ellie's right. We should all go to Disney this weekend. That's an excellent idea."

I almost choke. Since when is going to Disney *Ellie's* idea?

"Great, it's settled!" she says. "We'll take some time off and go together, like a big family!" She giggles so loudly that I clench my teeth. I can never, ever, *ever* let this marriage proposal happen.

Chapter 17

While Dad pays the check, I excuse myself and stomp down the hall to the bathroom.

I'm surprised the restaurant bathroom is one of those tiny single-person ones. I lock the door behind me and glance in the mirror, surprised at how terrible I look. My face is shiny and oily from the heat, and my hair is so limp that it could pass for black spaghetti hanging from my scalp.

Remembering how Carrie's head flip gave her hair more volume, I flip my head upside down and tousle my hair a little. Then I snap my head up, tossing my hair back.

Crack!

A weird sound echoes around me before the back of my head explodes in pain. Before I can figure out what's happening, I sink to the bathroom floor and everything around me goes black.

• • •

I wake up to the sound of pounding.

"Rachel? Are you okay?" Dad is yelling from somewhere far away.

As I sit up, my head is swimming. Why am I on the floor of a strange bathroom? And why is there blood on the tile next to me? And why does it feel like someone tried to saw my head in half with a butter knife?

I grab hold of the sink and manage to pull myself to my feet. When I touch the back of my aching head, my fingers come away bloody.

"Ah!" I cry, feeling a little woozy.

"Guard-doggit, Rachel!" my dad shouts, letting loose one of his goofy fake swears. "Open this door!"

Just then, the handle jiggles and unlocks. Ellie bursts in holding a key, my dad behind her.

"What happened?" Ellie cries while Dad's eyes go wide at the sight of the blood.

Ellie grabs a paper towel and quickly presses it to the back of my head. Then she has me sit down on the closed toilet seat.

"I was trying to...fluff my hair..." I say.

My dad and Ellie exchange looks like they think I'm delirious. "We need to get you to the hospital," he says.

Caleb peers in through the door while restaurant employees mill around in the hallway, looking in curiously. Now that my head is clearing a little, I'm more embarrassed than injured.

"No!" I say. Hospitals totally freak me out. Even though they always smell like disinfectant, I can't help thinking they're crawling with germs. "I'm fine."

Ellie pulls the towel away. "It looks like the bleeding is slowing down. But getting you checked out isn't a bad idea." For once she isn't smiling.

"Really, I'm okay," I say, getting up. "My head hurts a little, but that's it."

Dad looks to Ellie, who nods and says, "Follow my finger with your eyes, okay?" Then she has me do a few more things that I guess are supposed to tell her whether or not my brain is about to explode. I remember, suddenly, that Ellie used to be a nurse. Judging by how calm and reassuring she's being right now, I'm willing to bet she was a pretty good one.

"It doesn't seem like a concussion, and I don't think you'll need stitches," she concludes after inspecting the cut again. "But if you start feeling faint, we're going straight to the hospital."

"Thank you. You're the best," Dad tells her.

"It's nothing," Ellie says, but I can tell she likes the praise. My head pounds even harder.

Dad comes over and gives me a quick hug. "Roo," he says. Now that he knows I'm not dying, he looks a little angry. "Why can't you be more careful?"

I can't believe he's acting like I intentionally knocked myself unconscious. "It was an accident. I didn't mean to."

"You never mean to," he says. "But if you were more aware of your surroundings, things like this wouldn't happen. Then I wouldn't have to worry about you so much."

"If you were really so worried about me, why did you move so far away?" I snap. The instant the words are out of my mouth, I regret saying them. Maybe part of me means them, but mostly I don't. Things have been okay since Dad left, at least the past couple months. I'm not mad at him for leaving, not anymore. But it's too late to take back what I said.

Dad looks stunned for a minute. Then he lowers his voice and says, "We'll talk about this later." He gives Ellie a little nod and then storms out of the bathroom.

Caleb hovers in the doorway, clearly not sure what to do as Ellie works on cleaning the gash on the back of my head.

"Your father is—" Ellie begins.

"It's fine," I say, cutting her off. Ellie's known my dad for only a few months. I've known him my whole life. I don't need her telling me how to deal with him.

When we get back to the apartment, Ellie checks me out one more time to make sure I'm okay.

"Rachel, if you're not feeling up for work tomorrow, don't worry about it," she says. "We'll manage, okay?"

I hate how nice she's being to me. I might like her nurse side, but I can't forget about the other side.

My dad is quiet the whole time. Finally, he gives us a quick "good night" and announces he's heading home. He doesn't look mad anymore, just hurt. Part of me wants to apologize, but another part of me isn't ready to take back what I said. Maybe because it did feel somewhat true.

I can't help the sadness poking at my ribs. I thought coming here would help me reconnect with my dad, but if today is any indication, it's actually doing the opposite.

Chapter 18

I wake up early in the morning clutching my pillow like it's a life preserver. If these sinkhole nightmares don't stop soon, I might have to convince Dad to let me sleep standing up in his apartment after all.

My head still aches a little from yesterday's bathroom fiasco, but the bump on the back of my head is already half the size it was last night. From now on, I vow to be happy with my limp hair if it means never passing out in another bathroom again.

I have a few minutes before I have to get ready for work, so I go sit out on the balcony with my Gossip File notes. Even this early in the morning it's unbearably muggy out. I stare at the notes for a minute and then add to the one about Caleb. "Caleb's dad doesn't want him living there anymore, but Ellie's trying to hide it." I don't know if that's even gossip, but writing it down makes me furious. I hate that Caleb worships his dad when his dad doesn't even want him around.

Then a horrible thought creeps into my head. Am I fooling myself about my dad, just like Caleb is fooling himself about his?

No, that's impossible. My dad would never abandon me the way Caleb's dad abandoned him.

I shove the notes into my pocket and let my head sink into my hands. Why did I ever think coming to Florida was a good idea? Maybe I should call my mom and tell her I want to come home.

But I can't give up, not yet. My dad needs me.

After I get dressed, I head toward the café, my brain churning. As I walk past the Four Palms Salon, I spot Ellie inside, laughing and chatting with one of the stylists. I glance at the time and realize my dad is already at work. Something pings in my brain.

How would my dad feel about Ellie spending all that time not working while he's busting his buttons at his job? If I send him a picture of Ellie getting her hair done while he's lugging sandy equipment around, maybe that will get under his skin.

I stand in the window, trying to keep anyone inside from

seeing me. Then I hold up my phone and snap a picture of Ellie. The flash goes off, reflecting off the windows. The stylist turns to look outside as I leap behind a palm tree. Then I hurry away from the salon as quickly as I can.

Once I'm hidden in an alcove, I deliberate for a long time about what caption I should include with the photo. Finally, I say, *"Look who's getting all dolled up while you're at work!"*

I send it and hold my breath. A minute later, my phone beeps. *"Isn't she a beauty?"*

I almost throw my phone into the grass. How can I get my dad to see the truth about Ellie? I'm tempted to come up with some crazy plan to break them up, but there has to be another way. Every scheme I've been pulled into during the past few months has totally backfired, and I can't go through that again.

My brain is still spinning as I go into the café and fire up the ovens, eager to do some baking. When they're preheating, I take out the premade pastries and pop them in, but working on those just makes my baking itch worse, not better.

Carrie is wiping down tables and Taylor isn't here yet, so I start rifling around in the storeroom until I have enough supplies to make some muffins. As I start measuring and mixing, I instantly feel calmer.

After the muffins are in the oven, Carrie comes over, sniffing the air. "What are you making? It smells amazing in here."

"Chocolate chip coconut muffins."

"Those aren't ones we make, are they?" she says.

I shake my head. "I kind of made them up based on what we had. Don't be mad."

"Mad? Are you crazy? If this place smelled this good all the time, we'd be crawling with customers all day!"

"But I'm not supposed to make stuff from scratch. Ellie said Mark has it all figured out."

Carrie shrugs. "Who cares? As long as I get to eat one of those muffins, I won't tell anyone."

When Taylor comes in, she can't wait to get her hands on one, either. When they're finally cool enough, I divvy them up. Carrie practically inhales hers in one bite.

"Ava, these are crazy good!" Taylor says. "We should ask if we can make these for the café. Then we wouldn't have to worry about losing so much money."

I can't help smiling at the praise. At least the baking part of my life still makes sense.

"So are you finally done with your bits of gossip?" Taylor says.

I shake my head. "Almost. I'll have them done tomorrow." Since it's going to be my last day at the café, I figure I have no choice but to bring something in. I don't think the notes I have are anything the other girls will care about, but at least they'll see me—or Ava—as one of them.

The door opens and a group of customers comes in. More than half of them buy my muffins, which makes me feel good, even if it's technically against the rules. Once I break up Dad and Ellie, I'll be able to quit this job and then the rules won't matter anyway.

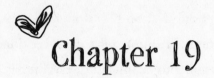

Chapter 19

As we close up the café for the day, I'm surprised to find Caleb outside in the grass, furiously gluing something together. When I get closer, I see that he's holding a few pieces of wood that look nothing like the trebuchet in his model.

"How's it going?" I ask him.

He shakes his head. "It's not working right for some reason."

"Do you need some help?"

He hesitates, like he's thinking about sending me away, but then he shrugs and says, "If you want."

I kneel down and glance at the model he's working from. "So you're making the base first, right?" I might not know much about building things, but I know what I'd do if this were a cake.

"I don't know," he admits. "I just started gluing things."

He laughs bitterly as he lets go of the pieces he's holding and they fall apart. "Maybe my dad's right. I'm not cut out for being an architect."

I have to chuckle. "You sound like me a few weeks ago. I was convinced that I wasn't meant to be a pastry chef, even though that's what I've wanted to be since I can remember. I was ready to give up."

"Why?"

"Because someone told me I was doing everything wrong. I thought that meant I didn't have what it takes. But it turns out, he was just trying to show me the right way to do things, and I was too stubborn to realize it."

Caleb shrugs. "Whenever I ask my dad for help, he explains stuff so fast that I can't keep up."

"So don't ask your dad," I say. "Maybe someone else can help you. Or maybe you just have to try things on your own until something works." I clap my hands. "Okay, let's start over and see what happens."

As we start gluing pieces together, the frustration on Caleb's face turns into intense concentration. Even if he's having a hard time with this project, it's clear that he loves building things.

"Have you ever asked your mom for help?" I ask.

He laughs. "Yeah, right. She'd just try to make everything perfect and ruin it. That's what she did with my dad."

My ears perk up. "What do you mean?"

"Dad works too much, so he's always late or has to cancel stuff. It stinks, but I guess I'm used to it. My mom took it really personally, though. The more she tried to make things in our family work, the worse they got. That's why she's so psycho with your dad. I think she's trying to make him the exact opposite of mine."

For a minute, I feel kind of bad for Ellie. Imagine trying your hardest to make things perfect and your husband still choosing work over you. I guess part of me can understand why she's been controlling my dad's life, but that doesn't mean she can just bulldoze her way through my family.

"My mom keeps trying to get me to move here," Caleb goes on, "but even though my dad works all the time, I'd rather be with him than with her. She only wants me around because she thinks it makes her look bad if her son doesn't live with her."

I think about that for a second as I spread glue on the end of a dowel. Should I tell him about the phone conversation I overheard? It doesn't feel like my place to say anything.

"I don't know if that's true," I say finally. "When your

mom told me that you lived with your dad, she seemed really sad about it. I think she really does miss you."

He shakes his head. "She misses telling me to tuck in my shirt and making me wear those stupid matching outfits. She thinks if something looks perfect, then it is."

He's right about the perfect thing, but I'm not convinced that Ellie doesn't care about Caleb. She might be a weirdo, but I think she really does want him around. Why else would she have gotten so mad about Caleb's dad abandoning him?

"She wasn't like that before," he adds. "Back when she was a nurse, she didn't have to try so hard to be perfect. I guess because she was actually pretty good at it. But ever since my parents broke up, she's like on this mission to be a robot or something."

"What about Amir?" I ask. "What happened with him?"

Caleb shakes his head. "I wasn't really around last year when all of that went down, but I guess his kids hated her because she kept telling them what to do."

"So she dumped him?"

"No, I'm pretty sure he dumped her. She moped around for months afterward, until she met your dad."

"Do you think…do you think our parents will get married?" I say slowly.

"I don't know. I like your dad, and my mom seems to really like him." He shrugs. "I think she likes the idea of us being one big family more than she'll like the reality of it, just like with everything else."

That gets something ticking in my brain. What if I've been going about things the wrong way? Instead of trying to prevent Ellie and Dad from being together, what if I could show Ellie what life would be like if we *were* a family? Would she still want to marry my dad if she got a super-dose of reality? Maybe she'd break up with him if she realized just how *imperfect* our family would be.

Caleb and I keep working in silence for a while until finally the pieces start to look like the model.

"This should probably dry for a while before you add anything else to it," I say, again thinking about what I would do if we were baking something instead of building it.

"Thanks," he says. "If I win, I'll give you some of the credit."

I laugh. "That's okay. You can take all of it. That way your dad will be really proud."

Caleb gets a far-off "if only" look on his face, and I find myself wishing things could be so easy for me. There isn't a competition I can win to get my dad's attention. It seems like no matter what I do, it's not enough for him to notice me anymore.

Chapter 20

As I wait for Ellie outside her office, ready to put my new plan into action, Mark rushes past me with a fire extinguisher.

"Is everything okay?" I call to him.

Marks slows down and gives me a weary smile. "Nothing to worry about!" he says. "Just a little mishap with a flaming baton."

"Can I help?"

He laughs bitterly. "Not unless you know how to teach a whole bunch of clueless people about Renaissance festivals. If someone asks you to host one, do yourself a favor and say no." Then he rushes away, muttering about how he'll never let himself be talked into any of Ellie's crazy ideas again.

I have to hold in my laughter. After how excited Ellie's been about this festival, it seems to be falling apart before it even starts. And clearly her boss isn't too happy with her right now. That makes two of us.

A minute later, Ellie's office door swings open and she marches out. She jumps at the sight of me standing in the hallway with a huge, fake smile on my face.

"Rachel, what are you doing here?"

"I wanted to walk you home from work," I say in my most cheerful voice.

She beams at me. "How nice! How's your head feeling today?"

Like it's full of thunderclouds, but I don't think that has anything to do with hitting it on the sink yesterday. "Great!" I say.

As we walk toward her apartment, Ellie chatters on about the Renaissance festival and how "super-duper" everything is going. After seeing how frantic Mark was a few minutes ago, I know it's all just wishful thinking.

"Of course," she says, "it would be better if I could find more than one jouster, but we'll make do!"

"Isn't the whole point to have two people jousting with each other?" I ask.

She laughs. "Traditionally, yes, but I think we'll still get the spirit across."

"You're totally right!" I say, even though I completely disagree. But I need to get her buttered up for what I'm about to say. I take a deep breath and add, "You know, I've been doing some thinking. I'm having so much fun in Florida that maybe I should move down here after you and Dad get married. You know, so I can live here for good!"

Ellie blinks at me. "Move here?"

"Yeah. That way I can be with my dad, and we can all be a family, and maybe we could even get a dog! One of those big, fluffy ones that plays fetch all the time and barks on cue."

"You'd really want that?" she says.

"Totally! We'd be the perfect family." I can't believe how fake this sounds, but Ellie seems to be eating it up.

"That would be great! Your dad would be so happy." Her smile falters a little. "I'm allergic to dogs, but I'm sure we can figure something else out. Maybe a cat? Or a hedgehog? I've heard those are popular pets these days."

Wow, is she calling my bluff or does she really think this is a good idea? Maybe I'm making this sound a little *too* perfect.

"I don't know if Caleb could live with us, though," I say, feeling like a jerk as the words come out of my mouth.

"I mean, I'm so used to being an only child that I don't think it would work to have both of us around. But he's moving back in with his dad soon anyway, right?"

Ellie's smile dims. "Well…"

"Great!" I say. "We'll have so much fun! I hope you don't mind if I use your kitchen all the time. I have to bake or I'll go crazy. Like lock-me-up-in-a-special-hospital crazy. But don't worry, I'm pretty good at cleaning up after my big baking marathons. We only got mice once at home, and that was only for a few weeks."

I don't even know what's coming out of my mouth anymore, but it seems to be working. Ellie's smile is gone now, replaced by the kind of frown you'd see on a cartoon character.

"Well, this is a lot to think about," she says as we finally get to her apartment. "I'll have to talk it over with your dad."

"You'll talk him into it, won't you?" I say. "Puh-lease?"

I can tell she feels guilty and put out, just like I've been feeling ever since I got here.

"I'll see what I can do," she says. As she hurries off to her room, I can't help the triumphant smile on my face. Finally, I feel like I'm fighting fire with fire.

● ● ●

I sit on the balcony with my Gossip File notes before dinner, trying to figure out what else to write. Finally, I find myself scrawling: "Mark hates Ellie for talking him into doing the Renaissance festival. He said it's the worst mistake he's ever made."

I stare at the words, realizing they're not really true. Mark was unhappy, sure, but he never said he hated Ellie. For all I know, he'll be over it by tomorrow.

Before I can erase what I wrote, there's a knock on the door. I shove the notes under the balcony chair and head into the room just as Ellie pokes her head through the doorway.

"Rachel, I have some good news," she says, coming to sit on the bed. "I spoke to your father and he agreed that you moving down here is a great idea."

"He—he did? I thought he'd still be mad at me after everything that happened at the restaurant."

She sighs. "He is a little moody at the moment, but you're his daughter. Of course he wants you to live with him." She gives my hand a reassuring pat. "You'll have to work out all the details with your mom, but if this is what you want, then we'd love to have you."

"But what about Caleb?"

"You're right that at some point he'll be going back to live with his dad. That's what he wants, after all." She frowns, and I bet she's remembering the conversation she had with her ex-husband. Somehow she's going to have to convince him to take Caleb back. "But in the meantime, I'm sure we can all figure out how to coexist, don't you?"

"I guess so."

"As for the pet hedgehog—"

"Dog," I say. "It has to be a dog. I know you're allergic, but a dog makes every family complete and perfect, don't you think?"

She thinks for a minute, and I start to wonder if maybe she'll finally crack. But then she nods and says, "I'm sure I can just take allergy medicine." She reaches out and squeezes my arm. "I can't tell you how happy I am that our family is finally coming together! Once I propose to your dad, it's all just going to be perfect."

Then she gets up and practically dances out of the room. I sit there staring after her, feeling like someone slapped me with a bowling ball. For the first time, it dawns on me that maybe this is one fight I can't win.

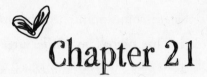

Chapter 21

I t doesn't surprise me when my dad calls that afternoon to say that he and Ellie are giving me and Caleb "the night off" so we don't have to meet them for dinner. He makes it sound like he's doing us a favor by letting us hang out by ourselves. Yeah, right. I can tell it's because he's still mad at me about our fight last night.

"Dad, don't you ever want some time to yourself?" I can't help asking before he can hang up the phone. "I mean, Ellie wants you to spend every second with her. Isn't that exhausting?"

He sighs. "Rachel, when you care about someone, you want to spend a lot of time together. Don't you feel that way about Evan?"

My cheeks grow hot. I'm definitely not used to talking to my dad about my boyfriend. "But Evan lets me do what I want. He doesn't try to control everything."

"Ellie is just particular, that's all. Your mother isn't much different, in fact."

I want to laugh as I hang up the phone. Yes, my mom can be a little psycho about details, like always wanting things to be clean and organized, but she doesn't smother us every second of the day. I can't tell if Dad really thinks that Ellie and Mom are so much alike, or if he's just telling himself that. But if he knows what Ellie is really like, why would he stay with her? Why would he let her tell him what to do? And, most of all, why would he let her get between us?

When my phone rings again, I'm afraid it's Dad calling to tell me he doesn't want to see me tomorrow, either, so I'm surprised to hear Carrie's voice.

"Hey, Kai and Taylor and I are going to get pizza later. Do you want to come?"

"Oh, I can't…" I start to say before realizing that for once I don't have any plans. In fact, why shouldn't I go out with them? "Actually, yes. Count me in!"

As I hang up the phone, I start getting really excited about the whole idea. Dad thinks he's punishing me by not hanging out with me tonight, but I'll be the one actually having a good time. I must admit that as much as I hate lying about who I am, being Ava has its perks. Rachel would never get to go out with a bunch of older kids.

Uh-oh. Except that I doubt Dad will let either Ava or Rachel go. He might not be nearly as strict as my mom is, but considering how much he complains about teenage drivers, I know he would definitely not be okay with me being in Carrie's car. My excitement deflates.

Just then, I hear Ellie whistling in the other room. Wait. Ellie!

I put on my most innocent face and go out into the living room. "Hey, Ellie. I was wondering if I could go out with some friends from the resort tonight. I tried asking my dad, but he wasn't answering his phone."

She blinks at me in surprise. "You've made friends here already?" she says. "That's great! Where are you planning on going?"

"Oh, um, some pizza place nearby." I have no idea if it's nearby, but I want to downplay the driving part. "Since I can't get ahold of my dad, I thought I'd ask you, since, you know, he values your opinion so much."

Ellie's skin seems to actually glow at the compliment. "Are you walking there?" she asks. "Do you need a ride?"

"No, um, I think I'm okay."

"Well, I don't see why you can't go. Your dad and I were planning to see a movie tonight, so you have the evening free. Just don't stay out too late, or you'll be tired for work tomorrow."

"Thank you, Ellie!" I cry. "You're the bestest!"

Then I do a little skip and triumphantly run off to my room.

• • •

"Hop in!" Carrie says, rolling down her car window. I always imagine high school kids having duct-taped clunkers, not shiny sedans that only look a few years old.

Kai is in the front seat, so I climb into the back with Taylor. Before I can even say hi to everyone, Carrie guns the engine, and we speed out of the parking lot.

As we whip around corner after corner, my stomach starts sloshing back and forth like I'm on a boat. Then we get to a stop sign, and Carrie slams on the brakes so hard that my tongue actually pops out of my mouth.

After that I close my eyes, too busy imagining fiery car crashes to pay attention to what Carrie is saying about the "ah-MAY-zing" pizza place that we're going to. My dad would have a heart attack, stroke, and brain hemorrhage all rolled into one if he could see me right now.

When we slam to a stop in the parking lot, I stumble out of the car on shaky legs, shocked that we got here in one piece. Would it be too bizarre if I begged Carrie to let me walk back?

The four of us grab a table in the corner as we wait for our pizza. As my stomach finally settles down, Carrie chatters on about pizza toppings while Taylor and Kai keep exchanging shy glances. Suddenly, I feel like my old mute self again. I can't believe I'm hanging out with a bunch of high school kids all the way in Florida. What the Shrek am I supposed to say to them?

Be Ava, I tell myself. *Be outgoing and funny.* But I'm too nervous.

Then Kai takes out a pack of cards and insists that we play a game. During the first round of a wacky Go-Fish-like game that I'm pretty sure Carrie made up on the spot, I barely say a word, my hands shaking every time I put down a card. But by the second round, we're all laughing so hard that the last of my nerves disappear.

I can't believe how comfortable I feel with these kids, like they're my real friends. Okay, yes, they think I'm someone else. But I feel more like myself with them than I have with anyone else during this whole trip.

"So, Ava," Carrie says when we finally give up playing her fake game. "Has Ellie told you what you're doing for the festival yet?"

"Does she have you practicing sword-swallowing or something?" Kai asks. "I swear, she's trying to kill us all. I'm pretty sure I saw Mark's tie catch on fire the other day."

"As long as the whole festival is 'perfect,' she doesn't care," Taylor says. She pitches her voice up to make "perfect" sound high and Ellie-like.

I let out a weak laugh. "Um, no. I won't be in the festival because I won't be working at the café next week."

"You won't?" asks Carrie. "But Ellie told us you were here for two weeks."

"I'm visiting for two weeks, but she said she'd find someone else to take over after tomorrow."

"Oh," Carrie says. "So what are you doing next week?"

"Going to Disney," I say. "If I survive it." And suddenly, as if the words are just waiting to burst out of me, I find myself telling them about everything that's been happening with Ellie and my dad. I don't tell them that Ellie is the mysterious woman I'm talking about—I just call her "the girlfriend"—but everything else is totally true. It feels good to finally share my real life with them.

When I mention that my dad's girlfriend is planning to propose at Disney, Taylor gasps. "But this is your dream trip," she says. "This woman can't just ruin it for you!"

At least someone else sees it the way I do.

"You know what you should do?" Carrie says. "When you're at Disney, don't leave them alone for a second so she can never ask him to marry her."

"But what if she does it when I'm there? I bet she'd want me to be part of it, just to make it even more horrible."

"Don't give her a chance," Taylor says. "Make it the least romantic day you can."

Kai laughs. "Yeah, if nothing else, feed both of them tons of garlic. That'll kill the mood."

I giggle as my phone starts ringing. I glance at the number and suck in a breath. Oh no. It's my dad.

"Hello?" I whisper.

"Rachel, where are you?" His voice sounds boiling-teakettle mad.

"I'm out getting pizza with friends. I told Ellie about it. You can ask her—"

"Come back to Ellie's right now," he says. Then he hangs up the phone.

● ● ●

On the drive to Ellie's apartment, I'm sweating like crazy, and it's not from Carrie's terrible driving or from the insane heat. I can't get over how mad Dad sounded.

I ask Carrie to drop me off at the end of the street, but she insists on bringing me right to Ellie's doorstep. Luckily, she doesn't realize whose doorstep it is. I rush to say goodbye and dart out of the car. But just as I'm about to make my getaway, Ellie and my dad come bursting out of the front door of the building.

"Whoa," Carrie says. "What's *she* doing here?"

My dad marches over to the car and yanks the back door open. "Rachel, get out here right now." I've never seen his face look so red.

"Dad," I say weakly.

"Rachel, now." Then he shoots Carrie and the others a scalding look before marching back over to Ellie, who puts a comforting arm around him. Together, they disappear into the building.

The car is suddenly totally silent as Carrie, Taylor, and Kai all stare at me in shock. Oh my goldfish. They heard my dad call me Rachel. They saw him canoodling with Ellie right in front of them. They know I've been lying to them. They know everything!

"Guys," I whisper. "I'm…I'm sorry—"

But Carrie cuts me off, her voice icy. "You better go, *Rachel*." She spits the name out like it's poison.

I climb out of the car and slowly close the door behind me. As I numbly make my way toward the building, I hear the car speed away.

My heart is pounding like a death-march drum as I walk up the stairs to Ellie's apartment. When I open the door, I find Dad and Ellie perched on the couch waiting for me.

"Sit," Dad orders as I shuffle into the living room.

I sink down into an armchair, not sure I'll ever be able to get back up.

"Where were you?" Dad demands.

"I told Ellie—"

"You told her you'd be going to a pizza place nearby with friends. You didn't tell me that your friend would be driving, or that she fancies herself a race-car driver."

"How did—?"

"I saw you leaving with Carrie," Ellie says apologetically. "When I saw how she drives, I was concerned, so I called your dad."

"How could you be so irresponsible, Rachel?"

I can't stand the accusing tone in his voice. "I wasn't

irresponsible! Ellie's the one you should be mad at. She's the one who told me I could go!"

"I don't care what Ellie said!" Dad cries. "You should have known better than to get into that car. You know I would never approve."

"But Ellie…," I say weakly.

"You got permission from Ellie because she didn't know the whole truth. She said you tried to call me, but I didn't have any missed calls from you. I don't know what's going on with you lately, but this behavior has got to stop."

There's nothing I can say to that.

"Go to your room," he says.

I stand up without a word and obey, but when I go to close the door behind me, Dad appears in the hallway.

"Ellie tried to tell me this trip was a mistake," he says from the doorway. "She said you weren't ready to handle seeing me with someone else, but I wouldn't listen. I thought I knew my little girl, but clearly I don't."

I stare at him. Ellie's the one who put all that "this trip was a mistake" stuff in his head? I can't believe it. She's been acting like she wants us to be this one happy family, but she's been poisoning my dad against me from the start. No wonder he hasn't wanted to spend any time with me!

"Don't think for a second that this kind of behavior can continue. Got it?" He sounds just like my mom.

"Fine. Sorry."

But I'm not sorry. In fact, I'm more determined than ever.

Chapter 22

The first thing I do when I get to the café in the morning is fire up the oven. I need to bake. It's the only thing that might get my mind off the fact that Carrie and Taylor are ignoring me and that my dad may never speak to me again. I walk past the disgusting premade stuff and start hunting for ingredients. Since it's my last day at the café, who cares if I break the rules? At least I'll make food that people will actually want to eat.

I make trays and trays of cinnamon rolls and muffins and tea cakes. The café is packed for most of the day. People can't seem to get enough of my pastries.

"Whatever you're doing with these things, keep it up," one of the resort lifeguards says as she bites into a cinnamon roll. "It actually tastes like cinnamon!" She laughs. "I'll definitely be back again tomorrow."

By the end of the day, all the stuff I baked is gone and the registers are practically overflowing with cash.

"This is the best day I've seen since I've been here," says Taylor, doing a little happy dance.

Carrie nods. "Definitely the best one we've had in years."

Neither of them looks at me.

I should be happy with how popular my pastries were, but I can't stand that my friends are still giving me the silent treatment. The only good thing about Carrie and Taylor being mad at me is that they've totally forgotten about my contribution to the Gossip File. But that doesn't feel like a relief at all. In fact, it feels like a punishment, like a sign that I was never really one of them.

Finally, as we're closing up the café in total silence, I can't take it anymore.

"Carrie? Taylor? I know you're mad at me and you have every right to be, but I really am sorry. I never meant to lie to you."

Taylor turns toward me, her face full of hurt. "Then why did you?"

"You guys assumed I was Ava, and after that, it…I guess it kind of spiraled out of control." I don't want them to hate me. I want them to understand. "The truth is, I liked being Ava. I liked starting over and being friends with you guys. I wished that I really could be her because it meant being able to hang out with you."

"So your dad is Ellie's boyfriend?" Carrie says. "And your name is actually Rachel?"

I cringe at the sound of her saying my real name. "Yes," I say, not able to meet her eyes.

"What about your boyfriend, Evan? Is he even real?" Carrie says.

"Yes! I can call him up right now if you want me to prove it."

"And the stuff about riding horses and having a farm?" Taylor asks.

I look at my toes. "Not true."

"Why would you lie about all that?"

"Because I'm an idiot! I should have just told you the truth right away, but I was too much of a wimp. And then it was too late." I swallow. "I know you must think I'm a horrible person. I'm as bad as Melody."

Carrie lets out a long breath. "No, you're not."

I look up. "I'm not?"

"Melody made stuff up to make herself sound more interesting than she actually was, but you're not like that.

I could tell you were a good kid when I first met you. You got caught up in some stuff. It happens to everyone."

"Really?" I say. "You're not mad?"

Taylor laughs. "We were, but I think we're over it. I mean, being mad doesn't undo anything, right?"

"You guys are the best!" I unclasp the horse necklace from around my neck and hold it out to Taylor. "Here, you should take this back."

"It's okay," she says. "You can keep it."

"No, really. I don't feel right hanging on to it."

I must sound pretty convincing because Taylor finally shrugs and takes the necklace from me. "I know what it's like to try to start over as someone new," she says. "One time after we moved I tried to go all goth. But after a while I started to miss the old me. And it killed me that I couldn't wear pink."

I shake my head. "The old me would never even be talking to you guys right now."

"Why not?" Carrie asks.

"Because I would have been way too shy to even say hi to you!"

"In that case, I'm glad you could be Ava for a few days," Taylor says, putting her arm around me.

My body floods with relief. "Thank you for giving me another chance after everything," I say. "I promise you guys won't regret it."

Carrie smiles. "I know we won't."

Chapter 23

As I'm getting ready for dinner that evening, there's a knock on the door. I'm surprised to see my dad standing in the hallway. I haven't spoken to him since last night. He doesn't look like he might explode with anger anymore, but he certainly doesn't seem happy.

"I thought we were meeting in the lobby," I say as he comes into the room.

"We were, but there's something we need to discuss." He closes the door behind him. Uh-oh. This can't be good. "The truth is, Ellie and I were talking, and we think that it might make sense to cut this vacation short."

I stare at him for a moment, sure I've heard wrong. "You're sending me home? But what about Disney? What about—?"

"After everything that's happened, it seems like the best decision."

I can't believe this. "Is it because of me going out in Carrie's car?"

"That and…" He sighs. "Let's be honest, Roo. Things haven't been going that well from the start. You've been arguing and making up stories, and just now Ellie told me that you've been breaking the rules at work. You didn't sell any of the pastries you were supposed to today."

"You're going to send me home because I *baked* some stuff at a *café*?" I practically shriek. "That's crazy!"

"There's also this." He holds out a piece of paper, and my stomach sinks right into the floor. Oh my goldfish. He has my notes for the Gossip File.

"Where did you get that?" I say. My mind starts racing as I try to remember the last place I put the notes.

"Caleb found it out on the balcony this morning. He showed it to Ellie, and they were both upset. Why would you write this, Rachel? What was it for?"

I could smack myself in the head for leaving the notes outside. How can I explain them to my dad in a way that won't sound terrible? "It wasn't for anyone. It was just…"

"Thanks to these notes, Ellie thinks Mark is mad at her for putting together the Renaissance festival, even though I tried to convince her that it's not true. And Caleb is barely speaking to Ellie because he thinks she's been lying to him about his father. Is that what you wanted? To hurt them?"

"No! I didn't mean for them to see it. I swear. Please don't send me home because of this."

Dad shakes his head. "I think we miscalculated with this trip. Maybe we can have you come down another time."

"But, Dad—"

"Sorry, Rachel. Ellie and I have talked it through, and we think—"

"Don't you see that this is what Ellie wants?" I cry. "She's the one who made you think this trip was a mistake. Once I'm gone, she'll have you all to herself again. She tells you what to do and what to think, and you do it!"

"Enough, Rachel! This wasn't Ellie's decision. It was mine." He storms over to the door. "Ellie's looking into flights home right now. I'll call your mother tonight and see what works for her. Chances are, you'll be flying back tomorrow." Then he leaves the room, and I stare after him in disbelief for what feels like an eternity.

● ● ●

That night, Ellie and my dad go out somewhere, leaving me and Caleb alone. When I go into the living room to watch TV, I'm surprised to see that, for once, Caleb isn't working on his model.

"Where's the trebuchet?" I ask.

He shrugs and changes the channel. "I gave up. It was stupid."

"What? But it was starting to look really good!"

"Who cares," Caleb says. "My dad thinks I'm a loser. Even if I win the contest, it won't make any difference. He still won't want me to live with him."

I sink down on the couch, feeling terrible. "I'm sorry you saw those notes," I say. "I never meant—"

"It's not your fault. It's my mom's! She should have told me the truth instead of pretending that my dad's assignment got extended and that's why he didn't want me to come home. If she'd told me what was really going on from the beginning, then I would have..."

"What?" I say. "Would you really have been okay with it?"

"No," he admits. "But anything's better than being lied to. She just wants to pretend everything is perfect all the time, even when it's all messed up!"

"She did it to protect you, you know." I can't believe I'm defending Ellie after everything, but it's true. She might not

159

be my favorite person, but she's a much better mom than Caleb gives her credit for. "I don't think she was trying to make things perfect. She just wanted to make them okay."

Caleb sighs. "Are you really leaving tomorrow?"

I nod. "My plane's in the afternoon."

"I wish you didn't have to go."

I stare at him in shock. Caleb's been so grumpy and wrapped up in his models the whole time I've been here. Why would me being around make any difference to him?

"My mom's been happier since you've been here," he explains.

"That's impossible. Your mom is always happy. It's my dad who's miserable, even if he doesn't admit it."

Caleb shrugs. "All I know is, she got really excited about going to Disney and going mini-golfing and stuff. She'd never do all those things normally."

"You know why she wanted to go to Disney? So she could propose to my dad."

He blinks at me. "Wow, really? Do you think it'll still happen even though you're not here?"

Ugh. With everything that's happened, I hadn't even thought of that. "I don't know. But either way, there's nothing I can do to stop it now."

"That's not why you came down here, though, is it? To stop them from getting married?" he says. "You just came to see your dad."

"Yeah, but once I saw how unhappy he was, I knew I had to do something to keep them from winding up together. Too bad it all backfired and now I'm getting sent home."

"So you're just going to leave like that, even though you and your dad aren't even talking?"

"What can I do?"

Caleb shrugs. "I don't know. But if I had a chance to make things better with my dad, I'd take it."

"What do you want me to do? He's sending me home tomorrow!" I cry. But I know Caleb is right. Maybe I didn't get my perfect Disney vacation, but that doesn't mean I can leave things the way they are. If I go home now, with my dad and me so mad at each other, we might never have a chance to be us again.

"Fine," I say. "I'll try to fix things with my dad if you still do the catapult contest. Deal?"

Caleb thinks this over for a second and then smiles. "Deal."

Chapter 24

Dad is already waiting in front of the café in the morning when I get there. I expect to be angry when I see him, but mostly I'm sad at how things have turned out.

"Hi, Roo," he says softly when I sit next to him on the bench.

"Thanks for meeting me."

"I can't stay long," he says. "There's a scuba trip going out in a half hour."

"Will you have time to take me to the airport later if you have a trip going out?" I can't help the bitterness in my voice.

"I'll manage. So what did you want to talk to me about?"

I want to tell him that I don't understand how things went so badly between us. I want to tell him that sending me home is the worst mistake ever. But what actually comes out of my mouth is: "How come we never have any Korean food or anything?"

He blinks at me in surprise. "Is this what you wanted to talk to me about?"

It isn't, of course. As usual, my mouth vomited out something without my brain's permission. But now that I've said it, I do want to know, especially since I might not have a chance to ask my dad about this for a while.

"One of the girls at work asked me about being Korean, and I realized I didn't even know any traditional dishes," I explain.

"Ah." Dad blows out a long breath. "I think that's partly my fault. When my parents came here from Korea with their families, they were both still kids, but they learned pretty quickly that being and acting different from everyone else wasn't the best idea, especially when you were Asian. It was after the Second World War, and if anyone suspected you were Japanese, well, you know…"

I shake my head because I really don't know. I remember learning that Japan was involved in the war, but when we talk about it in school, we mostly focus on Germany. And honestly, most of the time, I stare at the back of someone's head while my history teacher drones on and on.

"Let's just say it was better if people saw you as the friendly all-American neighbor," he goes on. "So, years later, after my parents met and married and had me, I guess it's not surprising that they raised me to be as American as possible. That meant only speaking English at home, only eating American food, and all that." He fiddles with the strap of his watch. "Now I wish I'd been more curious about where my parents came from."

It's strange that I've never thought about what being Korean actually means. For most of my life, it's meant not looking anything like my blond mom, dealing with judgmental people like the guy at the airport, and putting up with people asking me if I'm good at math. But the fact that my grandparents felt like they had to hide a whole part of themselves to fit in makes me sad. I know a thing or two about that myself. Maybe it runs in the family.

"Do you ever ask Grandma and Grandpa about it?" I know Dad doesn't see his parents much because they're all the way on the West Coast, but he calls them every couple weeks to check in.

"Not as much as I should," he says. "Next time I talk to them, I'll ask about Korean dishes, okay? Maybe you could even make us one sometime." He smiles at the idea, but then I watch his smile fade. He's probably thinking the same thing I am, that I might not see him again for months. "We'll figure it out," he adds.

I nod, but I can't shake the sadness sitting in my chest.

Dad glances at his watch. "Rachel, I really need to go soon. I assume there was something else you wanted to talk about?"

I nod, knowing I need to spit it out. "I want to apologize. I know I messed things up, even though I didn't mean to, I promise. I was so excited about coming down here, about hanging out with you again." Hopefully he'll see how sorry I am and change his mind about sending me home.

He sighs. "I'm sorry too. I know I'm partly to blame for how things have turned out this week. I was really looking forward to spending time with you."

"Then why didn't you?"

"Roo, you know I have to work—"

"That's not true!" I say. "You can get out of work to bring Ellie lunch, but you can't spend it with me? And why can't we ever do anything with just the two of us? This whole trip you've been making excuses and saying you want to spend time with me but not actually doing it!"

The words hang between us for a long moment. "I'm sorry if it's seemed that way to you, Roo. I guess I didn't realize how badly I was managing everything." He sighs. "The truth is, I was so busy trying to make everyone happy that I wound up disappointing all of you in the process."

I stare at the ground for a long while. "Dad, are we ever going to be okay again?" I finally ask.

He lets out another long sigh. "We used to get along so well. Now whenever we're together, we keep getting on each other's nerves. Why do you think that is?"

I remember what Marisol said the other day. "Maybe because we've both changed since you left."

He cringes at the word "left," like I've stabbed him with a toothpick. "I didn't leave you, Roo. Not on purpose, anyway. I hoped things would work out differently."

I know he means that he'd hoped my mom and I would have moved to Florida with him, but my mom refused to uproot our lives on one of his whims. At the time I was furious at her about that, but now I think she was right. What would we have done here? Lived in a tiny place with both of my parents scrambling to find jobs? Things at home are tight, but at least they're getting better. I don't know if I've ever seen my dad as down as he's been since I got here.

"Dad, please don't send me home. Not like this. I promise I'll try harder."

"Will you stop fighting me about Ellie?" he says. "Will you accept that I'm with her now?"

I bite my lip. I want to lie and say that I'll welcome Ellie with open arms, but the words won't come out of my mouth. Instead of answering his question, I ask something that I've been wondering since I first landed in Orlando. "Dad, are you really happy here?"

"What kind of question is that?"

"Because you don't seem happy! And if that's true, then what's the point? Why would you stay so far away from me if you don't even like it here?"

"Oh, Roo." He pats my knee. "Is that what you think? That I'd rather be here than with you?"

"Well, you *are* here instead of with me, aren't you?" I can't help pointing out.

"It's not that simple. Being an adult means making hard decisions."

"I'm sick of that 'being an adult' stuff!" I cry, surprising both of us. "If you really wanted to be home, you'd be home. It's that easy. If you want to be here, then stay here, but don't pretend it's because you have no choice."

"Honey—"

"I don't want to argue anymore. I wanted this trip to

be good, for us to finally spend time together. Instead, all you've been doing is working and acting like a totally different person."

"Roo, you don't understand what it's like to worry about money all the time."

I can't help it. I let out a honking laugh. "Dad, are you kidding me? I've done *nothing* but worry about money since you left! You have no idea how hard Mom and I have been working to stay in the house. I know you send what you can, and I know it helps Mom out, but it's not enough compared to how we were doing before you quit your old job. Don't tell me I'm a kid and I shouldn't have to worry about money and that I don't understand. I do understand! I wish I didn't, but I do."

"Rachel—"

"If you're happy here, then fine. Stay. But don't say I didn't warn you about Ellie, about you working too much, about everything. You talk about being a grown-up, about making mature decisions, but I don't think I'm the only one who needs to learn to do that!"

I jump to my feet and head toward the hotel.

"Rachel, we're not finished!" my dad calls after me.

But I'm done talking. I'm sick of feeling bad for

everything I do or say. I may not always make the best decisions, but I make them to protect the people I love. I wish I could say the same about my dad, but I'm not sure I understand him anymore. Maybe Marisol is right. Dad and I have both changed so much that it's hard to remember what we have in common.

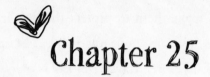

Chapter 25

As I shove my stuff into my suitcase, I keep replaying my conversation with my dad over and over in my head. So much for convincing him to give me another chance.

Maybe it's a good thing I'm going home. Coming here has made me lose my mind. I bet it's from the heat melting my brain. How else could everything have gotten so messed up?

I jump as someone knocks on the door. When I open it, I'm surprised to see Ellie standing there looking sadder than I've ever seen her. I would have thought she'd be bouncing off the walls now that I'll finally be out of her hair and she'll have my dad all to herself again.

"Can I come in for a minute?" she asks.

"It's your house," I say with a shrug. Then I go back to packing as she perches on the bed.

"Rachel, I wanted to ask you about the notes that Caleb found."

"I already said I was sorry," I say. "It was stupid of me to write that stuff down."

"But what were they for? I'm trying to understand how things went so wrong during your visit, and that's one part that just doesn't add up."

I sigh and try to think what to say. I guess I do owe Ellie an explanation since some of the stuff I wrote was about her and her family. "It was just for this stupid book at the café," I say. "All the new employees do it. You have to write down some resort gossip. I didn't know what to write, so I scribbled random stuff down."

"A book at the café?" she asks.

I shrug. Since I'm leaving today, I guess it doesn't matter if I keep the Gossip File a secret anymore. "Yeah, it's just some notes shoved into a book. It's not a big deal, and it's not meant to hurt anyone. The whole point of the book is to show that even though the resort looks like this perfect place, there's a lot of imperfect stuff going on there."

She gives me a long look. "Is the book a mystery novel?" she says, a hint of a smile on her face.

I put down the shirt I'm folding and stare at her. "How did you know that?"

She laughs. "Because I'm the one who started it when I worked at the café."

"You *what*?"

"It was years ago," she says, shaking her head like she can't believe how long it's been. "I'd just gotten almost-fired from my job answering phones, but luckily a spot opened up at the café. I hated it there, seeing all those couples and families coming in and out, laughing and talking together when I had no one. I'd just gotten divorced, and my own son didn't want to live with me. I'd left a good job as a nurse to work at a resort that didn't seem like a good fit for me. I was miserable, and I guess the only way I could make myself feel better was to write down all the not-so-flattering things I saw about those around me."

I stare at her, speechless. I can't believe Ellie started the Gossip File. "And did it help?" I ask finally.

She thinks about that for a minute. "I suppose it did at first. It helped get some of that frustration out, even frustration at myself. I don't know if you saw the notes about me in there, the ones I wrote."

I choke. "Wait, you're the one who wrote all of that stuff about not being perfect? Why?"

"Because it was true." She laughs. "It still is. But I think what helped me the most was showing the Gossip File to the other people at the café and getting them interested in it. After a while the gossip wasn't the point. All that mattered was that we had something to talk and laugh about together. It helped me to start trusting people again." She shakes her head in wonder. "I didn't realize that book was still there. I figured someone would have thrown it away long ago."

We sit in silence for a long while, and as each second ticks by, I feel worse and worse. "I really am sorry," I say. "I would never have written any of that stuff down if I'd known someone else would see it. I guess I was feeling pretty lonely too."

"You know, Rachel, I never meant for you to feel like I was taking your father away from you. I wanted there to be room for both of us in his life, and I think there can be."

She gives me a smile, and for once it seems real instead of the forced, perfect smile that she always puts on for show. I wish I'd gotten to see this side of her more often. Maybe then I wouldn't hate the idea of her being with my dad.

There's a knock on the door and Dad comes in.

"What are you doing here?" I ask. "I thought you had to go back to work."

He shakes his head. "I couldn't leave after what you said to me. It's been playing over and over in my head. And you're right. I've been so busy working and trying to make everyone happy that I've missed out on a chance to spend time with you. If you leave today, I know I'll regret it. So, will you stay?"

I blink at him. "Really? You want me here?"

"Only if you really want to be here, and if you swear that there won't be any more trouble. I promise I'll make more time for you from now on. My job can do without me for a few days. My family can't."

I throw my arms around him and squeeze as tightly as I can. "You won't regret this!" I tell him.

When I finally pull away, he wipes tears from his eyes. "So are we still on for our Disney trip?" he says. "I took tomorrow off."

"Yes!" I say.

"Great. And, Ellie, you can still do tomorrow, right?"

Ellie nods and squeezes his hand.

My excitement fades a little at the thought of her

coming with us, but I try not to let it show on my face. My dad's giving me another chance. I'm not going to ruin it this time.

Chapter 26

As we drive over to Disney World in the morning, determination pumps through my veins. Finally, I'm getting my trip with Dad. Okay, so I'm going to take Taylor and Carrie's advice and keep my dad and Ellie distracted all day so she doesn't have a chance to propose. But mostly, I'm going to focus on me and Dad having such a good time that he's going to remember why he asked me to come visit in the first place.

"Dad, remember my sixth birthday?" I say as we pull into the mammoth parking lot. "You said part of my present was that we'd come here one day."

He laughs. "You'd just seen one of those Disney movies about princesses, and you wouldn't stop talking about how much you wanted to meet them in real life."

"I'm glad we finally worked it out."

Dad smiles back at me from the front seat. "Me too, Roo."

"All the brochures say we should start in Tomorrowland," Ellie chimes in.

"I don't know why Disney has to have a Future World *and* a Tomorrowland," Caleb mumbles. "We get it. You want us to move on."

I'd been hoping we'd go to Epcot first, so of course Ellie announced we'd start with the Magic Kingdom. Dad swore we'd go later this week, though, so I'm not complaining. We park Ellie's car and go a million miles toward the ticket booths. The sun is so scalding that I'm surprised the parking lot doesn't turn into melted chocolate under our feet.

As we venture into Tomorrowland, I gawk at all the retro space-agey stuff. Everything is so big and shiny and colorful that I barely notice that I'm drenched with sweat.

We head toward Space Mountain, and I'm giddy with excitement. "I've always wanted to do this!" I cry.

"A roller coaster?" says Ellie. "I don't do roller coasters, do I, Caleb?"

He rolls his eyes. "No one's forcing you."

"In that case, I think I'll sit this one out," Ellie announces. "But you all go ahead without me."

I have no problem doing that, but my dad hesitates at

her "poor me" routine. "I'll stay with Ellie," he says finally. "You kids go ahead."

"What? No!" The whole point of us coming here is to do stuff together, and now Dad is going to send us off without him? Besides, I *cannot* leave them alone and give Ellie a chance to pop the question. "Let's find something we can all go on."

Dad gives me a long look but doesn't say anything. We keep wandering (and sweating to death) until we find a teacup ride in Fantasyland that Ellie's willing to try. Not exactly a thrilling adventure, but it's better than nothing.

We get in a line so long that I kind of want to cry. After waiting out in the heat for a while, though, it all starts to blur together. I'm so hot that I actually stop sweating. I wonder if that means my body is going into shock. Finally, we get to the front.

"I'll go with you, Teddy," Ellie says, but I'm already climbing into a teacup beside him.

"Ellie, why don't you go with Caleb?" I ask. She gives me a puzzled look, but she agrees.

"What's going on, Roo?" Dad asks as we start spinning. "Since when do you want to go on little kid rides?"

"I'm just trying to make sure we all have a good time."

Dad gives me a skeptical look, but he doesn't press. Instead, he actually starts joking around like he used to. By the time we get off the ride, I'm a little seasick but grinning like a monkey.

The rest of the morning goes great. We manage not to melt in the crazy heat as we wander from attraction to attraction. Every time Ellie tries to sit something out, I suggest another ride that she can't say no to. After a while, we check off pretty much every baby ride in the whole park.

When it's time for lunch, I order the biggest plate of garlic bread I can find and make sure Dad and Ellie both have a couple of pieces. Soon, we're all breathing garlic fire at each other, and I can tell Dad thinks I'm still suffering some long-term effects from my head injury. Surprisingly, I'm actually having a good time. Being with Ellie isn't nearly as bad when my dad is acting like his normal self.

I'm just about to suggest that we all get our faces painted when Caleb starts whining about not having done Space Mountain yet. After that, everything falls apart.

"Roo, how about you go with him," Dad says, "and I'll sit this one out with Ellie."

"But why don't we all go? It's really not that big of a roller coaster. Look at all the little kids going on it."

Ellie just laughs and shakes her head. "I don't think so. You two go ahead."

I stand there clenching my fists. What am I supposed to do now?

"Rachel, is there a problem?" Dad says.

I have to do something. I can't let her propose to him, especially not when my dad is finally starting to act like himself again. Desperate, I turn to Ellie and say, "Please, don't do it."

"Do what?" she says.

"Don't ask him, okay? He's not ready. I'm not ready. I don't think any of us are! Just please wait."

"Rachel, what on earth are you talking about?" Dad asks.

But before I can answer, Ellie's phone starts ringing. "It's Mark," she says, sounding concerned. "Why is he calling me on a Sunday?" After she answers it, she listens for a long, long time, her face getting paler and paler. Then she says, "Are you sure?"

When she hangs up the phone, her face is stony.

"What is it?" Dad says. "What's wrong?"

"That was the resort," says Ellie. "It turns out someone's been stealing from the café register again."

I stare at her. "What? How could some random person get into the register without us noticing?"

"No." Ellie shakes her head. "They think it was some-one who works there."

"Someone who works there?" I ask. "But who?"

Ellie looks at me. "They think it was you."

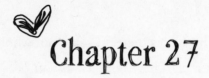

Chapter 27

My body really must be in shock from the heat. There's no way that what I thought I heard actually came out of Ellie's mouth.

"They said *I* took the money?"

Ellie nods. "It disappeared on the second day you were working there. Someone was going through the receipts and noticed it."

"But...but..."

"Of course there's some kind of mistake," Dad says. "But why would they blame Rachel?"

"Carrie and Taylor both said they saw it happen," Ellie says.

Now I *know* I must be hallucinating. "That's impossible! They couldn't have seen anything because I didn't do anything!"

"Maybe you accidentally—" Ellie begins.

"No! I didn't accidentally do anything. I didn't even touch the register the first couple days I was there."

My head is swimming. I stumble over to the bench and sink down next to my dad. I don't understand. Why would Carrie and Taylor lie like that? It doesn't make any sense.

"Didn't Melody get fired for stealing?" I ask. "Don't you think it's a huge coincidence that I'd be accused of doing the exact same thing a couple weeks later?"

"It is suspicious," Ellie says, "but the resort doesn't take these kinds of accusations lightly."

"We need to go back and straighten all this out," my dad says. "Caleb, we'll drop you off at home first."

As we walk back toward the car, my thoughts chase each other around like racehorses. What if the police really believe I took that money? What will happen to me? My mom will turn into a raging inferno when she hears about this. When we're in the car, I put my head in my hands, my temples throbbing.

"I don't understand how this could have happened," Ellie says, breaking the silence. "Why would those girls blame this on you?"

"I don't know," I say.

"Are you sure you didn't—"

"I didn't take anything!" I cry.

"Ellie," Dad breaks in, "Rachel is not a thief."

"It's just...considering everything that she's done since she's been here, I'm not sure we can trust her," she says like I'm not sitting two feet away from her. "I didn't want to worry you, Teddy, but I heard from Amir that she was harassing him at work the other day, and I think she even lied about wanting to move down here. It was all part of some game."

I can't believe she's saying this. "Do you know why I did all that stuff? Because of *you*, Ellie. Because of you forcing my dad to spend every free second with you. You've been suffocating him since I got here and making him miserable. No wonder he's been working so much. He probably wanted to get away from you. Today is the first day my dad's actually been himself since I got here, and it's your fault!"

"My fault?" Ellie echoes. "That's ridiculous! I've done nothing but support your father in whatever he wants to do."

"Rachel's right, Mom," Caleb jumps in, surprising me. "You always want to control everything and try to make things perfect. You did it to Dad and Amir, and you've been doing it to Teddy."

Ellie looks shocked as she sits back in her seat. I guess she's never heard Caleb be so honest with her before.

"Rachel," Dad says after a minute. "Is that why you think I've been working so much? Because of Ellie?" He lets out a sad laugh. "It has nothing to do with her!"

"Then why?"

"For you!"

"For me?"

"I already broke up our family," he says. "And because of me, you and your mom have been working much too hard. I realized that I can't let that happen anymore. I'm your father. I'm supposed to take care of you. That's why I want to make things easier on the two of you." He looks at Ellie. "And if I ever have another family, I want to make sure I can provide for them too. I'm never going to make the same mistakes again."

"But you've been spending all your time with her. You can't deny it!"

"You're right. I should have made more time for you, Roo. I guess I thought that if we were all together, then we could feel like a family again."

"But Ellie's not my family. *You* are, and you've been acting like you don't care about me anymore!" That's when the tears come. Big, fat tears that splash into my lap before I can stop them.

"Of course I care about you," Dad says softly, but I don't want to listen anymore.

Instead, I wipe my eyes and wait for the car ride to be over, dreading what will happen once we actually get to the resort. On my first day, I'd been convinced that Four Palms was heaven. Now, I'm just praying I'll make it out of there alive.

Chapter 28

The first person I see when we get into the hotel manager's office is Carrie. Her usual funny, laid-back persona is gone. Instead, she's nervously chipping away at her sparkly nail polish.

When she sees me, her eyes double in size. "Rachel? What are you doing here? You were supposed to be gone."

"Come on in," Mark says. "Shut the door."

I've never been called to the principal's office, but this must be what it feels like. Times ten.

"Where's Taylor?" I say.

"She had a family emergency," Mark says. "But I've already spoken with her. Her story matches Carrie's."

"And what exactly is her story?" Dad says. "Because I can assure you that my daughter would never steal anything."

"Let's hear what Rachel has to say, all right?" says Mark.

I nod and take a deep breath. Then I explain how it's impossible for me to have stolen anything since I didn't even touch the registers until my third day at work. When Mark asks me who I think might be responsible, I shake my head. Someone must have put Carrie and Taylor up to this, but who? And then I remember Carrie talking about how she doesn't have any money for college, which seems strange considering that she just bought a car.

Wait. Did *Carrie* take the money and blame me for it?

When I see the fearful look on her face, I realize I'm right. "No way!" I can't help saying.

Mark looks at me in surprise. "What was that?"

"It wasn't me! It was—"

Carrie furiously shakes her head, and I fall silent when I see the pure panic in her eyes.

"Rachel?" Mark says. "Do you know something you're not telling us?"

The pleading look on Carrie's face drills into me. How can she look so apologetic when she just threw me under the bus? I would never do something like that!

Except…maybe I would. After all, I've spent my whole trip lying to the other girls. But when Carrie and Taylor discovered the lies I'd told, they didn't disown me, even though they could have.

If I take the blame, my parents will be heartbroken. But

if I turn Carrie in… No, I can't. At least, not until I understand why she did it. She heard me out when I lied to her. I at least owe her that.

"No," I say through my teeth, shooting Carrie a look. Her shoulders sag in relief. "Only that I had nothing to do with that stolen money. I swear."

Mark clears his throat. "Well, Rachel, given all of this information, I must admit that your credibility is in jeopardy. Plus, we found this." He opens his desk drawer and takes out…my decapitated horse necklace?

"What's that?" Dad says.

"It was in the café register," Mark says. "This is another reason we suspect Rachel is involved with the missing money."

"You think that necklace is Rachel's?" Dad says. "That's ridiculous! Look at it. My daughter would never wear something so hideous."

"Actually," Ellie says softly, "I saw her wearing it the other day."

Dad looks at me for an explanation. "It *was* mine," I say, "but I…lost it a few days ago. I guess that's where it's been all this time." No doubt Carrie talked Taylor into putting that necklace in the register to frame me.

I glance at Carrie, but she still won't meet my eyes. How can she sit there and listen to all this and say nothing? Did the same thing happen to Melody? Is that why she got fired?

Mark sighs and says he'll be back in touch tomorrow. Then he hands me a paycheck for my week's worth of work at the café. Part of me is tempted to tear it up and throw it away. I had so much fun working there that I would have done it for free. Now I realize that my time there was as fake as my Ava persona.

As we leave Mark's office, Dad keeps his arm around me the whole time like he wants everyone to know that his daughter isn't a thief. Even Ellie gives me a sympathetic hug, which I guess means she believes me now.

"What happens now?" I ask.

Ellie sighs. "If we pay back the money that went missing, I should be able to convince Mark to forget about the whole thing."

"But that's not fair. I didn't take it!"

"Don't worry," Dad says, squeezing my shoulder. "We'll figure this out."

As we start to walk away, I'm surprised to hear Carrie calling my name. When I turn around, she comes up to me with her eyes cast downward. "Rachel, can I talk to you?" she asks, nervously tucking her hair behind her ears.

I shrug. "I guess." I turn to my dad and tell him I'll be right back and then follow Carrie to a nearby bench.

"I wanted to say thank you," she says.

"For what?"

"For not saying anything to Mark. I know Taylor's dad would kill her if he found out the truth."

I stare at her, not understanding. And then it dawns on me. "Wait. *Taylor's* the one who took the money?"

"Yeah, I thought you knew that, especially after you saw the necklace."

"But…but why?" The minute I ask the question, I realize how stupid it is. The first day I met Taylor she told me how much she and her dad were struggling. The whole reason she can't take ballet anymore is because she can't afford it.

"Taylor's desperate," says Carrie. "That's why I agreed to help cover for her."

"By blaming *me*?"

"You were supposed to be gone! When she admitted to me what she did, it was right after we found out you were leaving. I thought it would be perfect since we'd never see you again."

"Perfect? I might get arrested!"

Carrie laughs. "They won't do that. You're a kid."

"Is this what happened with Melody? Did Taylor take money that time too?"

She nods. "Taylor swore she wouldn't do it again after Melody got blamed. But right after you came, she found out that she and her dad were going to get kicked out of their apartment. She had no choice!"

"What about *my* dad? He works here. What do you think they'll do to him if they think his daughter is a thief?"

Carrie shakes her head. "It wasn't the best plan. I know that, okay? But Taylor was frantic. I had to help her. You're not going to turn her in, are you?"

I have no idea what I'm going to do. This whole day feels like a nightmare. I get to my feet and stumble out from under the shade of the tree.

"Rachel? Please, don't say anything. Taylor's your friend too, isn't she?"

"I don't know," I say, walking away.

Chapter 29

After my talk with Carrie, I wander around the resort for a long time. Everywhere I look, I see people laughing and enjoying themselves. Perfect families on perfect vacations. The sight makes me want to scream with jealousy.

But then I remember what Ellie said about starting the Gossip File because she was feeling exactly the same way I am. She wanted a reminder that the perfection around her was fake. And she's right. That adorable family by the pool looks like it's on the verge of a huge fight, and the laughing kids with their mom suddenly won't stop crying. What they have isn't perfect. It's just life.

I should have known that having Carrie and Taylor forgive me so easily for lying to them was too good to be true, but I wanted to believe it. I wanted to think that they were as amazing as I'd made them out to be. Maybe

I should have known better, just like I should have known better than to think my vacation with my dad could be the perfect trip I'd imagined when I was six.

Mom said that when she went on a trip when she was my age, she found out who she was. Have I found out what kind of person I am? I don't know. But I guess when it comes down to it, I don't want to be the person who lies about who she is and writes down other people's secrets. I want to be the kind of person who gives her friends a second chance, even if they might not deserve it, and who works to make things better with the people she cares about, even if it's hard.

When I finally get back to Ellie's place, I expect to find her and my dad still furious about everything that happened. Instead, they're both sitting at the kitchen table looking like they've been crying. Caleb, on the other hand, seems downright cheerful as he taps away on his iPad. Maybe Disney rubbed off on him.

"Is everything okay?" I ask. It's a dumb question considering the day we've had.

"Sit down," Dad says.

Suddenly I'm even more nervous. Are they going to announce that they're sending me home after all? Honestly, at this point it might be a relief to leave this whole joke of a vacation behind.

"We have something to tell you," says Ellie.

My stomach clenches. Oh no. If they say they're getting married, I'm going to dart out of Ellie's place and run all the way back to Massachusetts!

"Ellie and I have decided to…part ways," my dad says.

I stare at him. "Part ways?" I say, not understanding.

"They're breaking up!" Caleb says, sounding giddy. "And my mom's sending me to stay with my dad in Arizona! He said it was okay!" No wonder he looks so happy.

But I still can't believe it. Is my dad serious? He and Ellie are really over?

"What…what happened?" I ask.

They look at each other and then Dad says, "After we left Mark's office, Ellie and I had a long talk about some of the…points you brought up earlier, Rachel."

"Me?" I try to remember what I said. I accused Ellie of controlling everything, and I screamed at my dad that he didn't care about me. How did any of that make them decide to break up?

"I realized," Ellie says, "that I'm not ready to be in a relationship yet. I have some things I need to work on first."

"And so do I," Dad says. "I think for now we're going to be friends."

Caleb grins triumphantly at me. I should be happy too, but I'm not. Dad looks so miserable and so does Ellie. I guess she really does care about him.

"What happens now?" I ask.

My dad sighs. "We were thinking Ellie and Caleb might take a few days to head out to Arizona."

"Wait," says Caleb, suddenly panicked. "Mom, you're coming with me?"

Ellie looks a little pained, but she nods. "I think the three of us have some things to work out too. And after that, who knows? I don't know if the resort is the right place for me anymore. Maybe I'll go back to nursing." She turns to Caleb and tries to brush his hair out of his eyes. "Honey, why do you always have to hide your face? You're becoming such a handsome young man. I want to see it!"

Caleb flinches away, but I can tell he likes being called a "young man." I have a feeling it's going to take him a while to believe that Ellie really does care about him, but if they keep actually talking to each other like this, maybe they'll finally be able to work things out.

"Dad, Ellie, I'm sorry," I say. "For everything. I was only

trying to…" I laugh. "I guess I was trying to make everything perfect…and I just made everything worse."

Ellie gives me a sad smile. I guess she can relate.

Dad sighs. "I spoke to your mother earlier, and she and I agreed that because of some of your poor decisions during this trip, you'll be grounded when you get home. But for now, let's try to put all this behind us and spend some real time together, okay?"

I nod, wiping my eyes. "We used to do everything together, we used to be…"

"I know, Roo," he says, covering my hand with his. "We will be again. I promise."

And even though so many of my dad's promises have felt hollow recently, this time I believe him.

Chapter 30

The next morning, as I head off to check out the first day of the Renaissance festival, I find Taylor sitting outside Ellie's apartment. It looks like she's been slumped against the same tree for hours.

"Taylor?" I say.

She scrambles to her feet, her hair wild like she hasn't looked in a mirror in days. "Rachel," she says. "Um, can I talk to you?"

"What do you want?" I've decided not to turn Taylor in, but that doesn't mean I'm not still mad at her for letting everyone think I'm a thief.

"I wanted to tell you that I'm sorry, and I wanted to thank you. I know you could have turned me in yesterday and…well, I guess you still might have done it today, but it doesn't matter anymore."

"What do you mean?"

"I turned myself in," she says. "I told them the truth about Melody, and they said they'll give her the job back if she wants it. And I returned the money."

"What? But I thought you needed that money or you and your dad would get kicked out of your apartment."

She wipes her eyes with her perfectly tanned fingers. "I told my dad the truth, and he said we'd figure something else out. If we have to, we'll move back to Miami and live with my aunt. I'll miss Carrie and Kai, but if I get another job there, I might actually be able to take ballet again." She lets out a long sigh. "Hopefully my dad will start speaking to me again soon. He kind of hates my guts right now."

"Why did you confess?" I ask. "I wasn't going to say anything. You could have pinned it on me and been done with it."

"Because I realized how horrible I'd been! You would have never done anything like that to me."

"I lied to you," I point out. "I pretended to be a totally different person."

"Yeah, but you came clean about it. I realized I had to do the same thing, or I could never live with myself. The Melody thing was already killing me, and I didn't even like her all that much!"

"I know what you mean," I say. "Every time you guys called me 'Ava,' I felt like a total jerk."

"Can you imagine feeling that way for the rest of your life?" she says, shaking her head. "I told myself I was helping my dad, but really I was doing it so I could take ballet again. I thought if we didn't have to worry about paying rent, maybe there'd be something left over. It was stupid."

"If someone told me I could never bake again, I'd probably do some dumb things too."

Taylor brushes her hair out of her face. "That's another reason I couldn't let you take the blame for me, not after everything you did for the café."

"What are you talking about?"

"You haven't heard? Ellie insisted that Mark let the café make pastries from scratch."

"What? When?" I can't believe Ellie would do that, not when she worships Mark.

"Yesterday. I guess customers have been asking about your pastries for the past couple of days. One woman even told Ellie that the only reason she would ever consider going back there was because of them, since the rest of the food is horrible."

"Chocolate croissants shouldn't taste like garlic!" I cry.

Taylor lets out a dry, tired-sounding laugh. "I know. Heck, we all know. But I guess we needed you to show us how much better things could be. They're going to hire someone who can actually bake. Business has already picked up a lot since you've been here. I bet it'll be booming from now on."

"Wow." That's all I can really say. "Wow."

"Anyway, I'm sorry," she says. "I don't blame you if you never want to talk to me again, but I wanted to tell you that before I left."

"Thanks."

"You're thanking me? Why?"

I laugh. "I don't know." But I guess in some way I do. Because I may have been wrong about Ellie and Taylor and so many other things, but it's good to know there was some stuff I was right about too.

"Here," she says, digging around in her pocket. And, sure enough, she takes out the horse necklace. "I wanted you to have this back. Maybe it can be a good thing you remember about me instead of all the bad stuff."

I don't need an ugly necklace for that, but I take it anyway. "Thanks." I may never wear it again, but I'll always smile when I look at it. Besides, it doesn't seem quite as hideous now as it did last time I saw it. Maybe that means I'm becoming a horse person, after all.

• • •

After I hug Taylor good-bye and wish her luck, I head over to the resort to check out the start of the festival. As I walk through the tents filled with uncoordinated dancers and out-of-tune minstrels, I can't help smiling. Ellie might have had no idea what she was doing when she put this festival together, but everyone is having fun. Even if there is just one sad, lonely jouster riding around on what looks like a large dog.

I make my way to the catapult competition, and a huge smile spreads across my face as I see Caleb standing there proudly holding his trebuchet. He's surrounded by five other kids who are about half his age, all clinging to blobs made out of Popsicle sticks and pipe cleaners.

"Rachel!" he calls when he sees me. "I won! My trebuchet won!"

I laugh and give him a thumbs-up. He doesn't seem to care that the other kids who entered the competition are so young that they can barely spell their own names. And he shouldn't. His trebuchet looks perfect, exactly the way it did in the model.

"Your dad would be proud," I tell him.

"I can't wait to show this to him when I see him," he says. "I think he'll actually approve for once."

As I wander the rest of the festival, dodging out of the way of a group of clanging and creaking knights in rusty armor, I catch sight of Ellie standing in the middle of the festivities, looking horrified.

"This is a disaster," she says when she sees me. "It's awful! Look!" She points to a man walking by in a Chewbacca costume and a group of people dressed as Star Trek aliens. I guess no one told them this was a Renaissance festival and not a costume party.

"It's not so bad," I tell Ellie, but I can tell she doesn't believe me.

And then she does something I would have never imagined. She throws her arms around me and bursts into tears.

"I don't know what I did wrong," she sobs into my hair. "After all the work I put in, after how much I tried to make everything perfect…it just…it's all falling apart."

I stand there totally frozen. I feel an "at least it wasn't a shark attack" remark on the tip of my tongue, like the one that popped out when my mom was crying at the airport, but I bite it down.

What would Ava do? I ask myself. But then I realize that's wrong. No, forget Ava. She's not even a real person. *What would Rachel do?*

"It's okay," I tell her. "People are having a great time. See?" I point to a couple of giggling girls who just got their faces painted like purple cats and to a man proudly walking around with a sword he made out of a couple of sticks. "It's not perfect, but it's totally right."

"Oh, Rachel," she says, pulling away. "I wish you and I could start over. I think we're a lot more alike than we'd like to admit."

At first, that thought is horrifying. I'm nothing like Ellie! I mean, look at the way she tried to control my dad and make him do whatever she wanted. But then I realize... that's exactly what I've been trying to do for the past week. I guess I can't blame Ellie for wanting to make everything perfect when that's what I've wanted too.

Suddenly, a deafening siren starts blaring around us. The fire alarm. People stand in surprised silence for a second. Then they start to panic.

"What's happening?" Ellie cries.

"A sinkhole!" a woman yells nearby. "They say there's one near the building."

Oh holy artichoke hearts! My worst nightmares are coming true! Around us, kids run by screaming for their parents, stilt walkers topple over, and a couple of flamingos—where did *those* come from?—start jabbing at people as they pass.

I look around for Ellie, but she's disappeared, probably trying to manage the crowd.

Then one of the tents falls down and the whole scene turns into total mayhem. As I run blindly through the crowd, searching for Ellie and Caleb, I expect the ground to start shaking under my feet like in a disaster flick, but nothing happens.

Instead, a minute later I hear someone shriek, "My tree!"

I recognize the voice. When I push past a cluster of people, I see Ellie staring in horror at a hole in the ground where her dead orange tree used to be.

"My tree," she says in an odd, faraway voice when I go stand beside her. "I planted it my first day here…and now it's gone."

"It'll be okay. You'll plant another one," I tell her.

"No way," she says. "I hated that tree!"

"What?"

She laughs. "It started dying practically the minute I planted it. I've done everything I could to keep it alive, but it mocked me. It was a reminder of everything I was doing wrong." She wipes her eyes and glances at the hole. A work crew has already put orange cones around it. "Maybe now that it's gone, I can start to feel like myself again."

"Maybe we all can," I tell her.

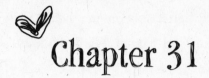

Chapter 31

A week and a half after I first arrived in Florida, it feels like my vacation is finally starting. As I wait at the resort for my dad to pick me up, Carrie keeps me company. We watch people splashing around in the pool. Kai sits at the smoothie stand as always, but instead of looking bored, he looks sad. I bet he misses Taylor already. I hope one day she'll be able to come back here. After all, the resort has given Ellie more than a few chances. Maybe they'll give Taylor a second one.

"So I wanted you to be the first to know," says Carrie. "I got rid of the Gossip File. I snuck up to the sinkhole when no one was looking and threw it in."

"Really? But you guys were so into it."

She shrugs. "Yeah, until it got you into trouble. Besides, knowing that Ellie started it totally weirded me out. It seemed wrong that it should still be around, especially if she's thinking of leaving the resort."

"I think you're better at making up games, anyway," I say. I'm definitely better at being me than at pretending to be some imaginary girl named Ava. I think we all let our melted brains get the best of us this past week.

"Go easy on Ellie, okay?" I add. "I know she's kind of intense, but she means well."

Carrie laughs. "Sure. You know, I think that festival kind of knocked her down a little. She seems more like an actual human now. It's nice."

Just then, Dad pulls up.

"Have fun today," Carrie says. "You earned it."

I give her a hug and then jump into the car.

"Next stop, Epcot!" he says, smiling. I keep expecting him to be depressed now that he and Ellie have broken up, but so far he seems okay. Better than okay, in fact. Maybe deciding to be friends really is what they both wanted. That makes me feel a little less bad about driving them apart.

As we go through the gate to Epcot, it feels like I'm really in heaven this time. There are no fountains or interconnecting pools, but I don't need all of that. Not as long as there's a giant, shiny golf-ball building in front of me, and I have my dad next to me.

Even the lines for the rides don't dampen my mood.

And the weather…well, it's not exactly cool, but either I've gotten used to the humidity or it really is better today. I feel like I can finally breathe.

As we wander around, Dad and I make up wacky stories about the people we see around the park. "Now that lady was definitely raised on a reindeer farm," Dad announces, pointing out a woman whose braids look a lot like antlers. We both laugh so hard, we're practically crying.

All the awkwardness between us is gone. It finally feels like I have my dad back.

As we wait in line for our next ride, Dad turns to me with a serious look on his face. Suddenly, my good mood dims. Uh-oh.

"Roo, I've been thinking about what comes next for all of us," he says.

"What do you mean? I thought you said Ellie was going out to Arizona with Caleb." Oh no. Has he decided to go with her or something?

"She is," he says, "but I've realized that with her gone, there's not much keeping me in Florida. I like it here, but… maybe it's time to start thinking about coming home for real this time."

I stare at him. "Home? As in *my* home? *Our* home?"

"It wouldn't happen right away," he says. "I'd have to keep working and saving up so I can afford my own place near you and your mom. But I'll only come back if that's what you want. Like you said, Roo, a lot has changed since I left. I can't expect to come home and think that everything will be the same."

I look at the ground, my head swimming. Of course this is what I want, isn't it? I've been dying for my dad to come home for months! But for some reason I'm not jumping and shrieking like I thought I would be. Maybe part of it is that my dad's talked about coming home before, and nothing's come of it. But it's more than that, I realize.

When my dad first left, I felt like my entire world had disintegrated around me. I thought the only way I could ever be okay was to bring him back. But somehow I managed to keep going without him and, bit by bit, to even be happy again. Of course I want him to come home, but I don't *need* him to. Not anymore. Either way, I'll be all right.

"I do want you to come home," I say slowly. "But if you decide to stay here, I'll understand. As long as we promise not to let things get messed up between us again, okay?"

He gives my hand a squeeze. "I promise, Roo. I've

already missed too much of your life. I don't want to miss any more." He smiles. "Once I'm back, maybe we can even find a Korean restaurant or two to check out."

I give him a long, long hug, like I'm making up for all the hugs we've missed over the past few months. "That sounds perfect."

As I finally let him go, I'm grinning so hard that my face actually hurts. I loop my arm through Dad's and drag him toward Future World.

Okay, so this wasn't the perfect trip I pictured when I was a kid. Mom isn't here, though she hates theme parks, so she's probably happier sitting this one out anyway. And Dad and I might not have checked off every theme park in Orlando, but just being here today is enough. Everything feels exactly the way it should.

And maybe someday, Evan and I will come here together. One thing is for sure. When I finally see him at the airport when I get home, I know the first thing I'm going to do. And it won't involve ears.

Acknowledgments

Eternal thanks to my family and friends, and to my EMLA, Sourcebooks, and Writers' Loft clans. I'm particularly grateful to Ray Brierly and Heather Kelly; without their help, this book would still be a vat of incomprehensible goo.

About the Author

Anna Staniszewski lives outside of Boston with her wacky dog and her slightly less wacky husband. She was a Writer-in-Residence at the Boston Public Library and a winner of the PEN New England Discovery Award. When she's not writing, Anna teaches, reads, and avoids cleaning her house. Visit her at www.annastan.com.

Don't miss the 1st book in
Anna Staniszewski's
new series

I'm With Cupid

June 2015

HE'S A CUPID. SHE'S A REAPER.
OPPOSITES ATTRACT.

The trouble all starts with a kiss. When thirteen-year-olds Marcus Torelli (who happens to be a supernatural matchmaker) and Lena Perris (who happens to be a soul collector) kiss at a party on a dare, they think the ZING they feel is just the power of a first kiss. It's only when they both get sent on assignments the next day that they realize their powers have accidentally swapped.

Now logical-minded Lena finds herself with the love touch, and ultra-emotional Marcus has death at his fingertips—and setting things right has become a matter of love and death...

RACHEL CAN'T BELIEVE SHE HAS TO GIVE UP HER SATURDAYS TO SCRUBBING OTHER PEOPLE'S TOILETS

So. Gross. But she kinda sorta stole $287.22 from her college fund that she's got to pay back ASAP or her mom will ground her for life. Which is even worse than working for her mom's new cleaning business. Maybe. After all, becoming a maid is definitely not going to help her already loserish reputation.

But Rachel picks up more than smelly socks on the job. As maid to some of the most popular kids in school, Rachel suddenly has all the dirt on the eighth-grade in-crowd. Her formerly boring diary is now filled with juicy secrets. And when her crush offers to pay her to spy on his girlfriend, Rachel has to decide if she's willing to get her hands dirty…

YOU KNOW ALL THOSE STORIES THAT CLAIM FAIRIES CRY SPARKLE TEARS AND ELVES TRAVEL BY RAINBOW?

THEY'RE LIES. ALL LIES.

I've spent my life as an official adventurer. I travel across enchanted kingdoms saving magical creatures and fighting horrible beasts that most of you think are only myths and legends. I've never had a social life. My friends have all forgotten me. And let's not even talk about trying to do my homework. So—I'm done! I'm tired and I want to go back to being a normal girl. But then along comes "Prince Charming" asking for help, and, well, what's a tired girl like me supposed to do?

Rachel's adventure continues

Operation save mom's cleaning business is a go!

Rachel Lee never thought she'd fight for the right to clean toilets. But when a rival cleaning business starts stealing her mom's clients, Rachel will do whatever it takes to save herself from the horror of moving to Connecticut—which would mean giving up her almost sort-of boyfriend, her fantastic new pastry classes, and her best friend Marisol.

But when the series of pranks Rachel and her BFF cook up to take down the competition totally backfires, Rachel worries that her recipe for success is a dud. You know what they say—if you can't stand the heat, stay out of the kitchen…